The sea is a cruel master. And Dominic Morgan, who has spent much of his life doing battle with it, as a yacht captain and commercial fisherman, explores its dark power in this tautly written collection of short stories with endings which pull you up short.
Sarah Pitt, Western Morning News.

Authentic throughout, Morgan's descriptions of the sea bring the reader close into the heart of his stories. He achieves brevity and beauty in Jumby Boat and the tension is built expertly in Passage to St. Maarten.
Kerenza Moore, Sunday Independent.

To Liz,
Love from Dom

DOMINIC MORGAN

BACKLINE AND OTHER SHORT STORIES

This book is dedicated to my children, Leon and Isabella. You are my salvation. My love for you is an ever flooding tide.
And to my mother and stepfather, whose love and support have got me through the hard times.

BACKLINE

I awoke with a start. Bloody Captain leaning on the horn. Dark. I stood up. Bathwater was cold now. I opened the window and leaned out into the frosty November air.

Let yourself in. Put the kettle on. I'll be down now.

I go into my bedroom and get ready. It's two-thirty. Bastard's never late. I make sure my knife is at the small of my back. Just so. I go down.

You're always late, Silas.

You're always on time, Calum. Where's my coffee?

We drink quickly and I have a slug of rum from the bottle on the kitchen table after he's marched out. Neaps moon. Less tide. Less work. I get into the truck beside my Captain. Six boxes of frames in the back. Cod and Haddock. Heads on, fillets off. Frames. Death ever present in our lives. The stench of it always around us. Always upon us.

Calum goes on board Curlew, I lift on the frozen boxes of frames and stow them abaft the wheelhouse to port. He starts the engine and I undo and throw on board the bow and stern lines and sternspring, I slip the forespring and go onboard. He motors forward on the forespring and Curlew's stern swings out into the channel away from the cluster of boats. We head out. I coil the mooring warps and stow them in the lazarette. Breakfast time.

As Calum makes way into the dark, I fry rashers and eggs. We eat in silence. Curlew starts pitching and rolling as we clear the point and head into the Atlantic to haul our first string. Forty pots on this one. An hour to drink coffee and smoke. An hour to split the frozen frames in two, to bait up.

Murdo was out early today.

I never saw him last night.

Aye, he's steady that one.

He usually has a pint, so.

Sure, he got in after us.

Did you see him so?

No.

How d'you know then?

You talk too much, Silas.

Ah, fuck yerself!

I don't like Calum. We steam into the gloom. I go aft and sort the god damn frames. I'm tired of this shit. We'd left the Broken Yard at midnight. Drunk. I'd had a hot bath. Fallen asleep in it. Woken up in cold water by a bastard captain taking me out to more bloody cold water. I wanted to wake at nine in the morning. Next to a beautiful woman. She'd be kind. She'd be warm. She'd like me for my smile and the guns this fucking work puts on my bones. She'd like me for who I am. Sure, and she'd be rich.

Seaway starts to build and I go forward into the wheelhouse to haul on my oilskins. I make sure I can get my knife out quickly. I check the edge. Keen as mustard, so. I replace the blade carefully. Death comes quickly at sea. He's always in the shadows. Watching. Waiting for a little mistake. An oversight. A psycho cousin that won't go away.

The little boat rolls violently as we're struck by a breaking comber. I'll have to watch the bloody backline today. Must check the stack before shooting the gear. One wrong step...

Calum calls aft to me.

Five minutes, set the sorting table and get ready with the gaff.

Aye, aye, yer rosy arsed bastard!

I unlash the parts of the sorting gear and set ready. I stand by the slave (we call the pothauler our slave) and peer into the gloom. Dawn is a hollow vow in the east.

I spot the dahn buoy before him, and tell him ten points starboard.

He comes aft to help me haul the gear. First the buoy, backline onto the slave. Hydraulics on. Up slowly, soon the chain. Heavy chain each end of the string. Stops the tide moving our gear too far. After the chain, the first pot. Parlour pots here. No escape for the crabs. Brown crabs this far out. Velvets close in. Maybe a lobster if we're lucky. Better price.

Hard work. Shake out. Sort. Bait. Stack. Then the danger. Calum forward to steam into the tide. Me aft amongst a hundred fathoms of backline, legs and bridles, all spliced to heavy pots to shoot into the dark. One wrong move...

The first string takes us thirty five minutes beginning to end. I'm sweating. Its ten minutes to the next string, so I go forward to roll a cigarette. Calum's already done it and hands me a steaming cup of coffee. I cheer up as I taste the rum he's poured into it.

What's that?

Ah, shit!

There's a blip on the radar. We head towards it. After a while we recognise Ann Bonney. She's turning circles around her gear.

We say nothing but exchange dark looks.

Calum radios but no response.

I'll put alongside to windward, go onboard and I'll stand off half a cable.

I climb over the gunwales between swells. The little boat's deserted. Marie Celeste in miniature. Murdo's half drunk coffee is on the bench next to the tiny gimballed stove.

I go aft and peer at the deserted deck. Scratch marks on the starboard gunwale. His knife rolling in the scuppers. No doubts now.

I go back into the wheelhouse and look at the

plotter. I set a course for the nearest string. Calum keeps pace half a cable away to port. I lay little Ann Bonney alongside the dahn and run aft to grab the gaff. I hook the buoy and lay the backline onto the tiny slave. Start hauling. Murdo works twenty pot strings.

It's a good haul. Four lobsters, eight big cock crab and thirty two hens by the thirteenth pot.

I throw them all overboard.

The thirteenth pot is empty. Deep breath. Steel myself for the inevitable.

He comes up after six fathoms of backline. Riding turn round his right sea boot. The leg broken. Bent the wrong way. Must have held onto the gunwale 'til it snapped. Scratchmarks on the gunwale, knife in the scuppers. Dropped it in his panic. Panic at sea means death.

Yeah, there were no crabs in the thirteenth pot. They were all on him. Eaten away his eyes and face. Put 'em all back, I did.

Got in early that day.

A big depression formed over us that night. We were stormbound for days. I drank all my wages.

HAMBLE

I arrive in Hamble at four. The village itself is quaint and medieval. On either side of it sprawl the various marinas from Hamble Point at the mouth of the Hamble River to Mercury Yacht Harbour further upstream where I'm due to spend the next four months.

I drive down to Mercury Yacht Harbour and park up near the Harbour Master's office. This is in a seventies block which has showers and a chandler's shop on the ground floor and a huge bar called "The Gaff Rigger" above. Hamble school of Yachting have an office at the other end of the hard, on which various boats and yachts are laid up on cradles for the coming winter. I pick my way through these to the office, enjoying the clink and rattle of the yachts' rigging tapping against their masts from the many pontoons that spread out from the hard into the river. The tide is flooding and the smell of ozone and brine fills my nostrils. I feel something like happiness seep into my belly like strong black rum. I feel like I'm home.

It is almost dark and although the lights are on, the office is deserted. I make my way back to the Gaff Rigger and climb the stairs to the bar. Inside is a large porch full of sea boots and oil skins. There is a door on the left to a large open air terrace and another on the right to the bar itself. I go into the bar.

The room is huge and takes up the entire length of the block. The bar takes up the length of the room. The drinking space is ten feet or so of standing room from the bar back towards the riverside and then rows of long tables that seat twelve or so people each all the way back to the floor to ceiling windows that look out over the river that is now filling with a thick fog with the incoming tide. The joint is packed with sailors and filled with the sound of laughter. A thick pall of cigarette smoke swirls above the crowd. I make my way through the crowd to the bar and await my turn to order. Presently a pretty blond girl gives the man next to me his change and smiles kindly at me.

You're new, what's it gonna be, Poppet?

Pint of Guinness, please, I reply with what I hope might be a winning smile.

Ooh, an Irishman, what brings you here?

She has the most beautiful smile and an irresistibly pert bottom. Her hair falls over her shoulders in thick blond curls and her skin is a lovely olive colour. I hope I'm not blushing.

Sure I'm after enrolling on a sailing course with Hamble School of Yachting. I can't find them in their office though.

What's your name?

Silas, what's yours?

Mandy. They're sitting over there Silas. She points at one of the tables. *You'll be here for a few months then?*

Four, I think.

Well, I look forward to seeing a lot more of you, Silas. She flashes me another smile and hands me my pint and as I make my way to the table, I am anticipating seeing a lot more of her.

There are nine people sitting at the table, three girls and six men. They look up as I stop by the head of their table.

Hello, I grin at them*, I'm Silas; I'm here for the Yacht Master course. Are you with Hamble School of Yachting?*

A stocky fellow stands up and shakes my hand. His brawny forearms are covered with tattoos; he has an all but shaven head and a long goatee beard.

He looks like a bloody pirate. He flashes me a warm smile.

I'm Matt, he says*, we're all here on the PST course, sit down and join us, Silas.*

I sit next to him and ask what PST is. He tells me it's for professional sail training and introduces me to the others. There is Lee Rogers sitting next to him. He's an unpretentious lad from Reading in his early twenties. Bernie Pratchett is a balding middle-aged salesman who I suspect is going through some kind of mid life crisis. He barely looks at me as he is intent on chatting up the young girl next to him. She is called Becky and is a plump blond with a posh voice and expensive brand new Musto sailing clothes. Next to her is a young lad of nineteen from Cornwall called Matt.

So we'll call you Goatee Matt and you Matty Cornish! I suggest with a grin. *After all if we're gonna be sailors we'll need nicknames so.*

This goes down well and they introduce me next to Lisa. She is twenty-one and from Liverpool. She has never been to sea before and is excited. Her long mousey hair is made up in tight dreadlocks and she's painfully thin. I reckon she may struggle, this one. Next is Sarah, a local girl who has worked for the school for some time to save up for the course. Danny Hogan is next to her and I think he is stoned. He says barely a word and looks like he hasn't washed for a month. Last of all I shake hands with Mark Burback. He is tall and thin and pale. Like Becky he too is very posh and has neither a chin nor an arse. I am not sure what to make of him.

We've been sitting and getting to know each other for ten minutes or so when a sturdy looking man comes over to the table. He has a ruddy face and a warm smile.

Hello, he says, *I'm Rob and I'm the chief instructor for Hamble School of Yachting.* We make room for him to sit down with us and go through the introductions again.

When we've finished our drinks, he continues, w*e'll go down to the office and victual the boats; you are all going to sea tomorrow for one week. This will be to get you acquainted with sailing a yacht. You'll be assessed during the week and will hopefully all pass your competent crew exam at sea. If not you won't be able to progress to the next stage which is your Day Skipper shore-based and then Day Skipper practical exams, so watch the drinking and study the manuals you will be given shortly instead of going to the pubs every night.* He grins but we can all see he's serious.

Tonight, he continues, *you will sleep on the vessels. They are both Sigma 38's which are great little yachts. Big Matt,* he nods at Goatee, *Lee, Silas, Mark and Becky will be on Pegasus which is on B pontoon. Bernie, Lisa, Danny, Sarah and little Matt,* he nods apologetically at Cornish, *are on Sea Pony which is tied up alongside Pegasus.*

Call me Goatee Matt, Goatee tunes him with a shy grin. *Big Matt makes me sound like a fucking porn star!*

We all collapse in fits of laughter.

I won't ask how that leaves you, little Matt. Rob grins, switching his attention to Cornish.

Well I'm never gonna get laid if you call me little Matt, everyone will think I've got a tiny cock! Better call me Cornish like these buggers here. He too is giggling and I know I'm going to like him.

Ooh, a porno star and a tiny cock, Lisa chimes in coyly, *the agony of choice!*

We finish our drinks and head down to the office. We're given our log books and competent crew manuals which list all the knots and manoeuvres we have to master to pass the exam. There is a diagram of a yacht and all its fixtures and fittings, and the parts of the boat, are clearly marked. I realise happily that this first part of the course will be a breeze as I learned the entire syllabus and more as a boy.

Each crew are then allocated a huge plastic laundry bag filled to the brim with our victuals for the week. We're not going to starve at least. Slinging our sea bags over our shoulders we make our way down to B pontoon. It's on the western side of the marina. I notice that Mark Burback has a solid suitcase instead of a sea bag and wonder where he's going to stow it. There are going to be five of us crammed into a thirty-eight foot racing yacht for a week and this nit-wit's packed a bloody Louis Vuitton suitcase.

Pegasus is a great little yacht with sleek lines and a narrow beam. She has a fractional rig which means the forestay doesn't reach the masthead so that the mast is raked back more which increases speed and her ability to sail close to the wind. I throw my sea bag into the cockpit and have a wander round her deck. She is well fitted out indeed and the forestay is bare so all our head sails must be hank-on rather than furling gear. This is good news too, as a furling headsail is less efficient for it loses its shape when you furl it in to reduce sail size when reefing in a blow. Everyone else has gone below so I go down to join them.

In the saloon Becky is busy bossing the lads around. She has Mark stowing the perishables into the tiny fridge in the galley. Goatee she has stowing the canned goods in the locker under the lower port coffin bunk. Lee is stuffing bottles of mineral water into the starboard locker. Goatee and Lee look up as I come down the companionway ladder and Goatee raises his eyes to heaven and makes a goofy face. Lee starts giggling.

What's so funny? Becky demands in her shrill, matronly voice.

Nuffin, says Goatee. Lee giggles again.

Come on, share the joke, I've clearly said something highly amusing.

Lee is now in hysterics and all but blowing snot bubbles.

Lee, I am going to ask you one more time, why are you laughing?

Sure, there's no harm in a laugh, Becky. I tell her with a grin.

You would do well to mind your own business, Silas. Now go and stow everyone's oil skins in the wet locker. It's on the left before you get to the loo."

What's a loo, Miss? I ask politely, holding my hand up. Even Mark is laughing now. She doesn't realise I'm joshing her.

You'd probably know it as a toilet, you ignorant bog trotter!

Oh no, Miss, we call that the head at sea. I flash her a cheeky grin.

Well put them in the wet locker next to the head then, honestly you are all quite exasperating!

Aye, aye Captain, I nod at her with a smile and do as she says.

The saloon is cosy with two coffin bunks, one above the other, both port and starboard. To starboard there is a table and benches screwed down to the cabin sole. The navigation table is aft and to starboard. Hundreds of charts are rolled neatly beneath it in plastic cases. Above, on the bulk-head are the instruments. A G.P.S. and the V.H.F radio, a compass and clock, a brass barometer and a boat speed indicator. There are two after cabins one to port and one to starboard. Becky will have one, obviously, as being the only girl onboard she will need her privacy changing and so on. I wonder who will have the other. My money is on Mark.

Who will sleep where? I ask Becky with a mischievous glint.

Well, I shall have one of the cabins and you lot can draw straws for the other, she says in her stentorian voice. I am beginning to warm to her. She's plucky and has plenty of character.

Would anybody mind awfully if I had the other? Asks Mark. *It's just that I suffer from a rather bad back and I'm frightfully concerned that these bunks in here will exacerbate the problem.* He looks hopefully at me and Goatee and Lee. I'd rather be in the saloon with the others anyway.

No problem by me, I tell him cheerfully.

Yeah, no worries, Mark, agrees Lee in his solid estuarine accent.

That's all right by me, says Goatee with a smile and he giggles, *but you realise you've just earned your nick name now.*

Which is? Enquires Mark.

Well, Mark Burback 'as a bad back, you're Bad-back Mark, Mate!

Very droll, says Bad-back, and stomps into his cabin with his ridiculous suitcase.

I ask Goatee and Lee if they want to come up to the Gaff Rigger. Goatee is tempted but reminds me that Rob was adamant we all stay on board and learn the three knots we need for this early part of the course. They are the round turn and two half hitches, the clove hitch and the bowline. I learned these when I was a boy. I suggest we take some line up to the bar and I can show them how to tie the knots there. It's much easier to be shown how to tie a knot than to attempt to learn one from a book. They agree cheerfully and we ask Becky and Bad-back if they want to come too. They both resist at first but Goatee reminds them we are crew now and must stick together and after a little persuasion they come.

There is no sign of the other crew so we get some beers and crack on with the knots. Goatee and Lee get them straight almost immediately but Becky takes a little while longer. Bad-back is hopeless and nearly two hours pass before he has them pat.

Goatee tells me he's from Brighton and is a keen guitar player. He asks me where I'm from. I tell him

I'm from Valentia Island opposite the Dingle Peninsular in County Kerry. My father Michael Murphy had a hotel there and three crab and lobster boats. I grew up going to sea with him and would sail those days we weren't at the potting. My mother was from Devon though, and had moved back there with me and my sister when I turned thirteen. She had left my Dad after finding him shagging one of the staff. She had fallen in love with a Scotsman soon after, and at fourteen I'd been sent to Gordonstoun School in Scotland. I'd still spent half of the school holidays with my Dad at home in Kerry and the rest of the time in Devon which I'd come to love even more.

It is eleven when the bar closes and we make our way back to Pegasus. The fog is thick and clammy and I'm happy to scramble into my sleeping bag in my bunk in the saloon. It's a wonderful change from the fishing. I zip myself up to the chin and pull the hood over my head. I talk quietly with Goatee and Lee for a while and then sink happily into a deep and dreamless sleep.

The next morning we get a rude awakening. A young man of twenty is standing in the galley banging a spoon on a saucepan. He has a very brown face and is a capable looking sort.

Good Morning all, he greets us cheerfully, *I'm Ben.*

I'll be your captain this week. Is anyone on any medication?

I'm bewildered and a little hung over.

I'm beginning to think so, I drawl.

We go through all the introductions again and he explains that if anyone of us is on any medication or has any allergies we should quietly let him know in private in case of any emergencies.

He tells us to fix breakfast and be on deck in our oil skins and sea boots ready to go in one hour. Becky wastes no time handing out the chores and we all sit down for a huge fry-up twenty minutes later. This kills our hangovers.

Becky sets Goatee and me the task of washing up and stowing away and we've just finished and are pulling on our oil skins when we hear Ben's heavy sea boots thumping along the pontoon. We go on deck as he climbs over the guard rail and he tells us all to put on our life jackets. He asks us to show him the knots we practised last night and I'm pleased to see that even Bad-back makes a good account of himself. Ben is clearly pleased. The other crew come on deck on Sea Pony which is tied up alongside us. Ben greets their skipper whose name is Jinks and I try to suppress a laugh as I realise what a deeply unsuitable name that is for a sailor. They start up their engine and after a prep talk by their captain we untie their mooring warps from our yacht's cleats, and they motor away down river into the fog.

We are made up to the pontoon but the tide is in mid ebb so Ben explains to us that until we get up some boat speed we won't have steerage way as our stern is pointing upstream. He tells us that we will leave the pontoon under power astern and then motor forward once we've cleared the pontoon. To help the yacht's stern swing out into the current, we release the fore and aft lines and the back spring line, then we power forward on the fore spring. The yacht's stern swings out, we motor away from the pontoon and then Ben throws the gears forward and away we motor downstream after the others. The fog is starting to lift now and a stiff breeze is getting up.

For the next few hours we take it in turns at the helm getting used to handling the yacht under power in the confines of the river. As we all progress we learn to moor up on the big empty pontoons in midstream and practise picking up mooring buoys. Ben is at pains to drum into us the names of the various parts of the boat and their function. He's a likeable guy and good at his job.

At lunch we tie up and wolf down some sandwiches and tea and are off again in half an hour. Ben explains how to raise the mainsail and motoring out into midstream we turn the bows to windward and raise the sail. Goatee and I go forward to hank on the number one Genoa and then haul it up on its halyard. We'd already tied the Genoa sheets onto the clew with the bowlines I'd shown them the night before, and Becky made up the other end of the working sheet to the primary winch. Goatee and I made our way back to the cockpit on the windward side deck as we made our way out into the Solent on a Beam Reach.

The rest of the day is spent practising the different points of sail from close-hauled to weather which has our rails under the water through beam reach, the most comfortable with the wind from the side, through broad reach on our quarter, and dead run with the wind behind. Everyone's picking it up quickly with the exception of Bad-back who is struggling and looking a little worse for wear despite there being precious little sea way in the protected confines of the Solent.

We moor up for the night in Cowes on the Isle of Wight.

After supper Becky and Bad-back stay behind to study their manuals, but both Lee and Goatee are natural sailors so the rest of us go to the pub. It's a great little place called the Ship, full of nooks and crannies. We find a spot under a poster of Neptune at Horta. The photo was taken during a hurricane and shows huge breakers crashing into the shore. One has broken on the Headland and looks like a face with a beard rising up out of the maelstrom.

The following day is spent practising man over board procedures under power, at first, and then under sail which is a damn sight trickier. Ben tells us we're going to stop for a snooze in the afternoon and then go for a night sail after dark.

There is no moon and the night is black as pitch with the thick cloud that's moved in from the south west. Ben points out the various lights of cardinal marks and channel buoys as well as those leading lights that show your way to the comfort of the many harbours. I sit silently on the windward rail and think about poor Murdo. This world of yachting is a million miles away from the hard life as a commercial fisherman. I feel guilty. I take a deep breath and fight back the tears.

The rest of the week sees us all well past the standard we need to pass our competent crew exam and after tying up once more on B pontoon in Mercury Yacht Harbour, Ben signs our certificates and happily hands them over for us to stick in our log books.

We spend a couple of hours cleaning Pegasus from stem to stern and take ashore our litter. I try not to laugh as Bad-back struggles back up the pontoon with his bloody suitcase.

Later we meet up in the Gaff Rigger with Rob who congratulates us on our week and puts us in the picture as to the next step.

Tonight you need to book yourselves lodgings for a week, he says. *There's a crew house not far run by Marion who's a great woman from South Africa. She charges ten quid a night and you sleep in bunk rooms. Tomorrow you'll attend your first aid course, next day's sea survival and radio after that. Then you have a day off and after that you're back here for your Day Skipper Theory course that will last one week. Then you get a weekend off before you go out for your Day Skipper practical which is another week at sea. You will be sailing to France.*

I'm thrilled and excited by this but even more so when I notice Mandy arriving to do a shift at the bar. She gives me a saucy wink as she walks past us and my heart skips a beat and my loins tighten with the knowledge she feels the same way. I go up to the bar when Rob's finished and the other barmaid, an elderly woman called Beverly asks me what I'd like.

Sure I'm just making my mind up, serve him while I think. I smile and throw a nod in the direction of a man a few feet further along. Mandy comes over seconds later.

Hello, Silas, you back ashore for a stretch then?

Ten days, wouldn't you know, I tell her with a smile.

How was the big voyage? She enquires, pouring me a Guinness.

It was wet and fun.

Wet and fun? I could do with a bit of the same myself!

That's easily arranged, Mandy. What time d'you finish tonight?

Eleven. She's flushed now and slightly short of breath.

Would you like to come on my boat?

She bursts into giggles and leans forward to

whisper in my ear. Her lips are warm and wet.
I'd love to come on your boat! She says in a low voice. I turn my head and give her a peck on the cheek.

I'll be back later then, I promise and return to the table with my pint.

After our drinks our crew clamber into my Land Rover and we trundle down to Marion's crew house a mile away. She's in her late forties and fun and friendly. She gives us a warm welcome and introduces us to her daughter, Jody who is very pretty and turns out to be Ben's girlfriend. I tell her he's been our skipper all week.

I know, she smiles. *He's told me all about you. How long d'ya all want to stay?*

Ten days, I think, but I may not be sleeping here tonight.

Why's that?

I've got alternative lodgings tonight, but I'll book my room anyway and pay for it, I just won't be using it tonight is all.

She's happy with this and so I pull Goatee to one side.

Hey, I tell him quietly, *I'm going back to the Gaff; you staying here or what?*

Nah Mate, I'm coming wiv ya! I wanna find Lisa, see if she 'ad a good week.

Right so, Goatee, let's split!

We walk back out into the drizzle and drive back to the Gaff.

Inside the bar the other crew have returned. They too have all passed their competent crew and are steaming through their drinks. By now it's nearly nine and I exchange winks with Mandy at every opportunity. At ten Goatee asks if he can borrow the Land Rover and I hand him the keys.

Pick me up here at seven tomorrow morning? I ask him and he grins, slaps me on the back and walks out of the bar with Lisa by his side, babbling sixteen to the dozen.

The bar shuts promptly at eleven and I catch Mandy's eye and point surreptitiously down stairs. She nods and I go down and wait for her in the shadows by the Harbour Master's office. Presently she appears and we kiss long and hard in the shadows. I take her hand and lead her down through the gloom to B pontoon. Pegasus is where we left her, pristine and creaking on her mooring warps, her rig making a merry tune against her mast in the soft night breeze. We climb on board and kiss again and make our way below deck to Bad-back's former cabin.

But poor Bad-Back's beaten us to it. He is lying naked on his bunk with a note in his hand. An empty bottle of pills rolls on the cabin sole. He's dead, of course.

BEANSIDHE.

Lee parked up outside the Chandlers and we walked up the hard to the yacht brokers. All the yachts on this part of the hard were forgotten boats. At some time they had symbolised the dreams of their owners but for one reason or another had ended up here, forgotten and abandoned, like unwanted dogs.

They sat in their cradles, their bows pointing hopefully to sea, their rigging tinkling against their masts, the rising Sou'wester moaning mournfully through their shrouds. A snapshot of futility. Goatee broke the silence.

She's over 'ere, Boys.

At the edge of the hard, just yards from the water's edge, a long-keeled sloop sat in her cradle. She was utterly forlorn and needed a great deal of work but we saw immediately her potential.

We walked slowly around the hull, tapping it with our mallets. It seemed tight. No cracks. No blisters. No signs of osmosis. The propeller needed replacing as did her anodes. This was a good start and I began to feel excited. There was a ladder against her port quarter padlocked to the guard rail. We climbed up and went on deck. The boys went forward to check the spars; I started aft with the backstay. We spent an hour checking the standing rigging and then another forty minutes scrutinising the stanchions, guard rail and running rigging. Then we went below into the cabin to talk it through.

Mast's been painted to hide the pitting. Said Lee.

Bottle screws are cracked and the chainplates want replacing. Added Goatee.

I'm going to buy her, boys! She's perfect.

Goatee and Lee go through the inventory and check the electrics while I go to the Brokers to make Charlie an offer. After some haggling we agree on twelve thousand as seen and I wire a third of my life savings into the firm's account. Beansidhe is mine. Never before have I been so excited. I return to the little sloop to tell my friends and already as I cast my eye over her something about her has changed. A boat is a living thing and needs to be loved and cherished like any woman. She knows I have bought her. She knows I love her.

She knows it is just a matter of time before she returns to the sea. A gust of wind blows over her and she gives a joyful shriek as it passes through her shrouds.

I climbed onboard to join the others. We'd passed our final Yachtmaster exams the month before in February; I had told them I was in the market for a little yacht as I meant to sail over to the Mediterranean and then later the West Indies. We were all working now as freelance skippers so had agreed to keep our eyes skinned collectively to find something suitable. It was Goatee who had found her and we'd all agreed to take some time off work to make the necessary repairs on the condition that we'd sail her together to sunnier climes.

Flash, at Performance Rigging, had found us the mast and boom and spars that we needed and we spent a couple of weeks swaging the new bottle screws to the stainless steel shrouds we'd ordered. We spliced up the new halyards and jib sheets and replaced the engine.

Over the weeks, of course we found countless other minor faults that we repaired little by little. Sometimes Goatee and Lee would disappear for a week to go to sea on contract. We were all on a tight budget. It was July before Beansidhe was ready to be hoisted back into the drink and have her new mast fitted.

This took place without mishap and finally she lay on a pontoon, bobbing happily on the brine, pristine and new; a jaunty rake to her mast.

I waited there for a week for the boys to come ashore and join us.

All these weeks I slept each night in her main cabin on the starboard coffin bunk. It was like a workshop below deck but cosy and I'd fitted a little gimballed stove so I could cook onboard. I slept well all this time, partly due to the hard work. But there was something else too. I felt reassured on her. Like she was looking after me somehow. I dreamt each night that I was at sea on her and my dreams were vivid. It was as if she were whispering to me. Gone were my fierce memories of the fishing and the death that stalked me there. I felt reincarnated. Reborn. Beansidhe spelt security and liberty.

There was little for me to do when the work was complete but wait for the boys. I victualled the yacht and filled her water tanks. I sanded down her grab rails on the coach roof and applied twelve coats of varnish. I thought about taking a little contract at sea but I couldn't bear the thought of being away from her. I was dying to take her out to sea but remembered my promise to Lee and Goatee, so waited impatiently for them to return.

The night before they came ashore an old gentleman came down to the pontoon. He was trim and wiry with a silver beard. He wore navy blue moleskin trousers and a Guernsey sweater of the same colour. His eyes were deep blue like mine and had a mischievous twinkle. His eyes smiled even when his mouth did not.

He introduced himself quietly and told me that Beansidhe had been his yacht for thirty years.

She was built by Holman and Pye on Canvey Island in 1967, he told me, *and I am truly delighted she has been purchased by somebody who knows his business. You have done a first rate job fitting her out, young man, she sorely needed attention and it pained me to watch her rot in that cradle these past four years.*

Why ever did you let such a fine yacht go? I asked him quietly.

He was silent for a moment while he gave the question his careful consideration.

We all of us grow old, if we're lucky enough. It creeps up on us. I circumnavigated the globe three times on my dear little Beansidhe but one day I awoke and had suddenly become an old man. My circumstances changed. Sadly, she had to be sold. It broke my heart and hers, I believe, though I can see you have mended that also and I am pleased for the fact.

I invited the old man onboard to closely inspect all the many changes and repairs we had so carefully and lovingly made over the months. He was delighted. He inquired where I was planning to go with her and was thrilled when I told him. He assured me I would find her an excellent sea boat and very forgiving. He reluctantly left after an hour and casting one final loving look at her he walked away down the pontoon into the gathering twilight.

The next day, the boys came ashore and we made ready to go to sea. My plan was to run a couple of hundred miles west of the Lizard and then put Polaris on the backstay and head south for La Corunna. This route would keeps us well away from the shelf at Ushant. The Bay of Biscay has a fierce reputation so I wanted to cross it in deep water where the seaway would be more tolerable should we encounter a gale. I went into the bar for a pint before we set off and saw old Charlie from the Yacht Brokers. I went over to buy him a drink and say farewell. I'd finished mine and was on my way out when I suddenly remembered that I'd forgotten to tell him about Beansidhe's former owner coming to visit and look her over the previous night.

He gave me a peculiar look and told me that Beansidhe had been sold four years earlier because her owner had died. Lung cancer, apparently.

ANCHOR CHAIN

Beansidhe lay on a mooring at Puerto Andratx, in Mallorca. I took one more look at the forbidding sky and hauled on my gear. I was going to check the swivel at the base of the mooring. Only four fathoms of water. No decompression stops. The tramuntana was coming.

There was a hairline fracture in the swivel so I replaced it quickly. Back on board and out of the scuba gear. I untied the dinghy painter and pulled her up under the bow. Put all three anchors and the chain and warps into the dinghy. Then climbed down into her and carefully set them out so they lay in an arc to windward. Back to the yacht and back into the scuba gear.

It took another forty minutes to dive down and bed in the anchors. Back on board I hauled up the slack on the rusting capstan. Then fitted some nylon warps as bridles to the anchor chain. This would stop the fierce snubbing on the bow when the katabatic wind struck later. All set, nothing to do but wait now.

There are seven other yachts in this part of the outer harbour. They are deserted. The wealthy yachties have fled for the safety of the sheltered marina. Thirty euros a night. Nothing to them. I haven't the money, of course. I am out here on my own.

I walk back along the side deck to the cockpit and slide back the old teak hatch. The salt has turned the teak white over the years. I climb down the companionway ladder into the warm glow of the main cabin. Everything's been stowed away but my knife and the bottle of Mount Gay rum. I put the sheath knife on my belt, always in the small of my back. I sit at the chart table and drink my rum in the gathering twilight.

The tramuntana is a katabatic wind here. It accelerates as it gallops down the steep mountains into the bay. It comes without warning. The halyards' ting tinging against the mast increases slightly in tempo and volume then a hundred knots of wind crashes into you like the Devil himself, intent only on your destruction.

It is the noise that overwhelms. As the wind hits the stainless steel rigging it screams as it gusts and moans as the wind speed decreases between the gusts. Sounds like revenge. Nature's revenge for our rape of her. It is the noise that plays on your nerves. It is this screaming that fills you with the primal fear. It is important to control this fear. A mistake in these conditions spells death. It is the end if you panic.

The storm comes like a thief in the night and rages for seven hours. I spend the night in the cockpit. I am shielded from the worst of the elements by the coach roof. Two of the other yachts, a sloop and a yawl, break their moorings and are carried away to the rocks. They're dashed to matchwood.

I do nothing to save them. I fear for my own boat. I fear for myself. I fear.

A couple of hours before dawn the wind abates slightly and backs into the east. In this moment a third boat snaps its mooring. A large catamaran. An expensive charter vessel. It drifts quickly towards the other side of the bay. Towards the town quay.

A thought occurs to me.

I quickly go below as it takes shape and steel my soul with the rum.

The salvage on a boat of this class would pay a pretty dividend. With my heart in my mouth I run to the foredeck and unlash the dinghy. The wind tries to rip it away but I get her over the side and tied off to the transom.

It's a tricky business but I manage to get the outboard safely onto the dinghy and fit it quickly to the back plate. She starts immediately and slipping the painter I chase after the catamaran through the waves. I am moments too late. She strikes the rocks to seaward of the town breakwater before I can get a line on and tow her to safety. She is holed immediately and begins to sink.

Suddenly three figures emerge from the gloom and hasten down the rocks to the floundering catamaran. One by one they leap onboard. Dangerous business that. If they mistime the jump and land between the rocks and the yacht they'd be crushed to pulp. All three make it onboard swiftly.

Throw me a line.

I shout this at the top of my lungs and the smallest of the three sees me.

Shot, China, catch!

He's South African. I catch the line and slowly, slowly tow the big catamaran away from the rocks. I tow her back to the sandbank a cable away to seaward. I hold her over the bank and she settles on the seabed in a couple of feet of water. Perfect.

There is an argument going on onboard. I tie the dinghy off to the leeward hull and go aboard. They are debating who has salvage rights. I join in. Of the four of us onboard, one man, the largest, watches us others from the safety of the afterdeck.

We three are on the trampoline. A catamaran has no foredeck. The two hulls are connected here by netting that stretches over and above the water beneath and is made up to the hulls with bungee. It bounces as you walk on it. Trampoline.

Both the other men are South African. Yarpies. All three of us believe we individually own the salvage rights. They each argue they were first onboard, I argue that it was me who pulled the vessel to safety. One of the Yarpies is big, the other tiny. They are both powerfully built and aggressive. The fight starts as quickly as the storm and with as little warning.

The big Yarpy has a dangerous right but is slow. I get a couple of good shots into his jaw. The little one is quick but his punches don't carry. We are bouncing on the trampoline as we fight which makes it hard to be accurate. The smaller guy apologises when he hits us in the balls. At this point I get the giggles. We stop fighting and agree to split the salvage. I get back in the dinghy while they get the hook and chain out of the anchor locker. After twenty minutes the boat is secure on her sandbank.

We make our introductions. Both the men are called Nick; we call the smaller one Zulu which he tells us is the name of his sloop. Just then we are joined by the fourth man. He is Dutch, called Dennis and manages the boat for a charter company. He tries to claim salvage but thinks better when we fall silent and fix him a steely glare. We all go ashore to sign a contract and get the tools we need.

It takes us four days to repair the hole and pump the hulls out. To fit the floatation bags beneath the hull was the hard part. There wasn't enough room between the hull and the seabed to wear the scuba gear. We had to lay the tanks and regulators fore and aft and grab a breath as we lashed the bags along the hull. It was ok when the swells were under the boat, but as they receded the boat would sink and press you into the seabed. We'd have to wait for the next swell before we could breathe. It was the danger that made us brothers.

On the day we finished we sorted a tow and got her over to the hoist. We went to the charter company's office to get paid. No sign of Dennis. On honeymoon they told us. We'd just have to wait.

We were tired and sore and disappointed. We went to Bergman's to drink rum.

* * *

Three weeks went by. No money. We began to get antsy. The boys collared me in Tim's bar one afternoon. I was in my cups.

We'll draw straws, brew!

This was Zulu. Nick nodded and we drew the straws. I knew they'd set me up before I drew but I loved and trusted them so I let it go. Nick looked at me.

You're the Patsy, Silas! Be on Beansidhe by half past three tomorrow afternoon, say nothing when Dennis comes. If he gives you the money you can speak. We'll take care of the rest, China!

They take off so I drink the rest of my money and return back to Beansidhe caned.

As I'm doing my checks before turning in, I open my anchor locker. It is empty. Twenty fathoms of galvanised chain...gone!

The rage builds up inside me so I go below and settle in the cabin at the table. The bottle is empty but the glass is full. I correct the glass and fall asleep where I'm sitting.

The following day I rise at dawn. I put the coffee on the stove and dive naked into the glassy sea from the pulpit up forward. The water envelops me and the joy returns. I swim around the little boat and then climb out as I hear the coffee squeal. Crouching on the starboard coaming I sip the scalding cup and smoke a cigarette. I'm intrigued to see if that bastard Dennis will show later.

I spend the day splicing an old mooring warp to the spare chain I keep in the lazarette, and making some minor repairs to various breakages I suffered in the tempest. At quarter to four I hear a RIB approaching. I notice it's the same as the one the men were using yesterday but Dennis is alone at the tiller. He stops alongside Beansidhe's port quarter but doesn't cut the engine.

I've got the money...cash! Are we okay?

I can't believe my fucking ears.

I don't speak. He cuts the engine. He's clearly quite terrified.

I'm going to take the money out and pass it to you

to count, ok?

I look at him but I promised the men so still say nothing. Dennis is pale and counts out the dough with shaky hands. His fingers are thin and straight. No breaks in his life this fucker, I watch him count the money...six thousand in fifties...then he hands it to me. I fold it and put it in my pocket. The pocket's barely big enough! I'm allowed to talk now but can't think what to say.

Silas, I'm sorry, I'm so sorry. You have the money now...please tell me we're okay.

I'm totally fucking bewildered.

Of course we're ok. I tell him. He relaxes.

So I don't need to worry?

You don't need to worry about me or the men but I want you to shit off now.

He starts up the outboard and speeds off to the town quay. I count the money again. Six thousand. How the fuck did they pull this off? I wonder as I climb down into my dinghy to go find them and split the dough.

I find them in Bergman's. They look up at me as I

walk in. Their faces are a mixture of hope and trepidation. They say nothing so I put 'em out of their misery and haul out the huge wad of cash. They reach out to grab it but I cuff both in the head and fix them a hard glare.

Nobody gets a cent 'til you tell me how you did it!

Their faces light up with mischief and they both pummel me for a while.

Zulu spills the beans after a while.

It was easy, Brew! We stole your anchor chain yesterday and put it into Dennis's RIB. Then we went to find him. We told him if he didn't have the cash by four today and put it in your hands, he was a dead man. We explained that you had decided to wrap him in that anchor chain and take him out to sea. We told him that you reckoned gravity would take care of the rest!

SHANGHIED

Bergman's was filling up. There were few stools vacant at the huge horseshoe bar. All of the tables were taken. Nick and Zulu had pitched up at Beansidhe earlier. It was Zulu's idea.

You've been out here for six months. Tie up on the Town Quay for a bit. Two euros a night, Brew! Have a break, fill up with sweet water! Shot, China! We'll get caned! Spend some of the salvage dough...besides; it's St. Patrick's Day-let's celebrate!

I couldn't think of a reason why not. They wanted to go to Bergman's but I was feral after eighteen months aboard. My sea boots had died and my T-shirt was dirty. I had a pair of linen strides but had cut them off below the knees to save the rips spreading. We would be the scruffiest men in the bar and doubtless the ugliest by far.

Maria, the owner of Bergman's, was a kind Austrian lady. She loved us a little I think. Whenever the three of us went in there she would bring us a plate of whatever she'd been cooking. She knew when we had money we would pay. When we hadn't she would give us the food. She did a roaring trade with the wealthy tourists and the Tupperware phonies. The well-heeled and the beautiful filled her coffers each day. We were her pets. She called us her sea gypsies and in return we loved her as dogs love their mistress. We made her laugh and if anything broke we would fix it.

This night, however, we had the salvage plunder in our ragged pockets and we meant to spend it. We sat at the bar laughing and joking. We traded stories of our adventures and even engaged the yachties. We were in our cups when my life's tide turned.

The door opened and in she came. She was beautiful, it's true, but there was something else. I think now it was an atmosphere, an aura that enveloped her. I only know that I was unable to take my eyes off her. She was not alone, of course. A girl like that never is.

The man beside her was handsome. A pretty boy. The bastard looked like Johnny Depp. He was well-built and muscular. Those muscles had been made in a gym, though; not carved onto him by the rigours of seatime. They were for show, not for purpose.

The men noticed.

Eh, Zulu! Does Silas seem a bit quiet to you?

Yar, China! I wonder why!

Maybe he's overcome by all these posters of Ingrid Bergmann.

Yar! Or maybe he's thinking how he's going to spend the salvage dough!

Could be something else, though.

Could be! Do you think he's noticed that lakka, lakka girl who just walked in?

I can't listen to this anymore.

There's no justice, Boys! Would you ever look at her! Ah Jaysus, I think she's seen me, so!

You are a pussy! This came from Nick. *Not weeks ago you risked your life each day with us but you don't have the courage to talk to her!*

It's true, Brew! You are not normally so shy, why now do you lose your bottle? Are you frightened of Johnny Depp?

What am I to do?

GO AND GET HER!!

They shouted these words in unison. They looked a little bewildered for that fact, then smiled again.

I rise from my seat and walk over to her, our eyes have met and time is frozen.

* * *

I know he's seen me. I know this. His eyes are blue like the sea. More so because his skin is so brown. This is no tourist. He is not ugly, exactly, but there is something about him. He and his friends are different. They are all different. It isn't just their dirty, torn clothes or their deep tans. Nor is it their obvious strength. Their musculature is different from David's. It has been torn into them.

My sister introduced me to David yesterday. She said I would like him. She told me he looked like Johnny Depp. He too is Belgian. It is our first date tonight. A blind date. So far he has talked about himself non-stop. He is very good looking, of course, but dull.

But these guys are different. There is something about them. Something dark! Something compelling!

I know which one wants me. It is the one with those sea-blue eyes. The three seem to be equals but I think he is in charge. The other two love him but I sense he doesn't know love. That is my impression.

Oh God, I think he's coming over. Our eyes have met. Those eyes, I'm transfixed by them. There is something else behind them and I think its danger or the knowledge of it. Yes, he knows danger, this man. He's closer now and his eyes don't leave mine for a second.

He moves slowly with confidence. I think he's a sailor. He doesn't walk like you or me. It's a slow, rolling gait. I know I am here on my date with this beautiful David; but it is this strange man who has suddenly made me wet.

I'm Silas! His voice is deep and lyrical. I think he might be Irish. He gently picks me up, effortlessly, by my barstool as if I am a Tapa he is about to eat. He carries me over to his friends on the other side of the bar. They are grinning wolfishly. David follows but not for long.

Silas holds me in his left arm and pulls the barstool away with his right. He puts it on the ground between himself and David. He speaks slowly and quietly.

If you follow us, Horse, I'm going to hurt you. Then my men will eat you. Best you go now while you can so.

I'm shocked how quickly David backs off. Only ten minutes ago he was telling me how he was a black belt in karate. He scuttles off to the door like a frightened rabbit. He doesn't stop for his drink, an expensive cocktail. He just runs, like a rabbit! I can see Silas's men sniggering, but Silas himself is silent.

He puts me down gently next to the others and fetches my stool from where he left it. A posh yachtie has made to take it but he quickly hands it over to Silas. The men are called Nick and Zulu. They are very funny and pretend to fight over who will buy me the first of many drinks.

We talk and joke for a couple of hours but Silas doesn't say a word. Finally he asks me if I'm hungry. I smile and say that I am. He suggests we go back to his place to eat a curry he made earlier. *He wants me.* We leave. We arrive at the Town Quay after five minutes' walk and he explains that he lives on a boat. It is a beautiful little yacht on the end of the quay. I need no persuading to follow him onboard. I take off my shoes. I wonder if he will kiss me or ask to kiss me. If he asks I will like him less. I needn't have had the thought. He goes below into the cabin ahead of me and as I climb backwards down the ladder his hands are on my legs.

He pushes up my skirt and presses his stubbled face between my buttocks. I arch my back and push myself onto him. His hot, wet tongue devours me. The unbearable heat starts deep within me and I come violently and uncontrollably on his face in a series of frantic convulsions. Only then does he pull me into the cabin and push me roughly over the galley table. He slides his swollen cock slowly into me from behind. The other boys always want to make love with me. Maybe that is why I have only slept with girls these past two years. But this is different. This is primal. It is bestial and urgent. This is not love but furious nature stripped raw. We fuck each other until we are spent and then he carries me into the forward cabin which is one giant bed. We fall asleep entwined under the full moon's ghostly light that pours into the cabin through the forehatch above us.

When I awake we are no longer on the Town Quay but at sea under sail. The land is a smoky smudge on the horizon and we're sailing east into the rising sun.

TRAMUNTANA

I turned the bow to seaward and went forward to drop the hook in three fathoms of water. Laid out fifteen fathoms of chain. Plenty of scope. Then I rigged a bridle. I looked up at the heavens. Mackerel sky. Cirrus. I remembered my old captain's mantra. High feathers, heavy weathers. To seaward the sky was changing already. Thick cumulus on the horizon. Dark prophets, denizens of the storm.

There were three other yachts at anchor here in the inner harbour at Andratx. Battered blue water boats. The charter boats and the Tupperware phonies had fled to the safety of the marina. No doubt they'd be propping up the bar and spouting tall stories while we coped at anchor. At least I wasn't at sea.

I knew the other two yachts. Zulu and Gitana. The third I hadn't seen before. She was a beauty, her American ensign fluttering behind her in the strengthening breeze. I think she was a Herreshoff, wooden, sleek lines, good sea boat.

I got in my dinghy and did a turn around her to get a closer look. Nobody on deck. She was called Silverwind. I went ashore to buy provisions and to stock up on rum.

Sophia was waiting for me at Bergman's. We had a quick lunch of tapas and returned to Beansidhe before the storm struck. She was feeling low. Monthly courses. She went below to curl up on the big bunk I'd built in the forepeak.

I stowed the outboard and lashed the dinghy to the foredeck. Nothing to do but wait.

The first gust hit us at five that afternoon. Strong Katabatic wind racing down the Tramuntana range. Seventy knots of howling gale hit us like a broadside. The wind howling through the rigging, the rain cold, heavy, relentless.

I went below to check on Sophia. She looks like a child when she sleeps; pure, ethereal, untainted by the passage of time. I kiss her gently on her lips and go back on deck.

Conditions had worsened and the visibility was poor. I glanced at the plotter to check the anchor hadn't dragged but the heavy CQR had dug into the seabed like a plough and Beansidhe danced on the gathering swells.

I leant in through the companionway and switched on the C.D. player. I left the deck speakers on but switched off the ones in the cabin so as not to disturb Sophia. She'd bought me a new harmonica for my birthday. Blues harp in C. I wanted to play along to the original Fleetwood Mac line up. Had their "blues jam in Chicago" sessions. Nobody to hear me make a pig's ear of it in this weather.

I had a swig from the rum. I like storm spent at anchor. The atmosphere is heavy and electric before the storm. We too feel the same. When the storm breaks and unleashes its fury, we too are released and it feels good. There's no past or future in a storm. We live moment to moment. We become existential. We become real. But most of all we become alive and that is the thrill.

I heard the dinghy before I saw it. A tiny drone half drowned by the pent up rage of the storm. I peered anxiously into the gloom. My eyes stung from the salt. I watched in disbelief as a tiny dinghy appeared on the crest of a wave then vanished altogether in the trough.

Within a few minutes I had a constant visual. He steered his dinghy with great skill. Pure Zen. Once within a few yards of us he steered round to leeward and paused in the slick water there. He was silver-haired and had on only shorts. He was steering the outboard with his left hand and clutching a guitar with his right. There was a bottle tucked into his belt. He grinned and shouted up.

Hey Man! I heard you playin' the blues so I came over to join in. Permission to come aboard?

I reckon you earnt it! Here throw me the painter!

I tied her off to the leeward after cleat and helped him onboard.

We shook hands.

Name's Jimmy.

I'm Silas.

Nice boat you got here, is she a Holman Pye?

He had a southern accent and was soaked through. His chest was bare and covered in scar tissue. He'd been badly burnt at some time. I was surprised he knew who'd built my Beansidhe.

Yeah, strider 36! She was the first of four. Is yours the Herreshoff I was admiring this afternoon?

Sure is!

She's a beauty, you sail her all the way from the States?

Sure did!

Single-handed?

Yup.

Well let's have a rum and hang out, I'll get you some dry clothes.

I brought up a sweater from the cabin and we sat under the awning stretched over the boom. I lit the storm lantern and lashed it under the boom. I was curious about the scarring and wanted to hear more about the enigmatic old man.

How d'you get all those scars? He didn't seem fazed by the question but paused for a sip of rum before answering.

Well I was all blowed up in the war, man! Vietnam. I went out in '69 when I was nineteen. Phosphorous grenade. I was one of the lucky ones. They sent me home. I'd never seen the sea before my tour. Once on the way to war and once again when they flew me home. I was raised on my Daddy's farm in Kentucky. Well he died a few years back, so I sold up the farm and bought myself that boat and a sailing manual. Now I'm here!

I was dumb with admiration and stared at the old

guy in total disbelief. I filled our glasses while I took it all in.

So you never sailed before?

Nope. I figured it out on the way. I ended up in Greece. Met a girl, married her, now we on our way back to the States.

Where's the girl?

She don't feel good. She's sleeping.

Mine too.

We drank rum and played the blues until dawn but the storm was still not spent. We finished the rum and had a strange conversation before he left. He told me he believed we all had a limited time that the sea would allow us to be safe. He reckoned sooner or later she took everyone. Then he said something really strange. He told me he could see a hex on me. Said he used to see it on some of the men in his platoon. The ones who would die. Told me I shouldn't push my luck. Then he left.

By ten the following day the storm had blown herself out and Sophia and I went ashore to get some breakfast. I was surprised and disappointed to notice that Silverwind had already gone. I'd told

Sophia all about Jimmy and the strange night we'd shared.

We met up with Nick and Zulu at Tim's Bar for ham and eggs. They fell quiet as I told them all about Jimmy. Their faces went pale. There was a pregnant pause. Nick broke it and there was fear in his eyes.

Silverwind got sold last year, Brew. The American drowned. Fell out of his dinghy on his way out to her in that big Tramuntana last year. It was before you got here. His girlfriend was inconsolable. She committed suicide.

PASSAGE TO ST. MAARTEN

You are Captain Murphy?

The question is yelled belligerently in a thick accent, Polish or Russian perhaps. I look down from the masthead where I'm replacing the yacht's tricolour running lights and spy a huge man peering up at me from the pontoon. He has a pale freckled head like an anaemic cannonball and squints up at me through the bright Caribbean sunshine. He is built like a silverback gorilla. His hands are clenched on his hips. I snigger as I consider the various facetious replies available to me.

I know.

I have boat you must deliver to St. Maarten. I will pay you two hundred dollars. We leave tomorrow!

What sort of boat?

Beneteau 44, very good boat!

It's a Tupperware box!

What you mean?

Its okay for floating around here but no good offshore in heavy weather and it'll be fierce tomorrow, be sure of that!

He doesn't seem to be too pleased with my enthusiasm.

Bullshit! Is very fine yacht, cost hundred fifty thousand dollar!

His big bald pate is turning puce.

Ever played poker?

Yes.

Well then you'll know if you can't spot the idiot at the table, you're it!

There is a pause as he considers this little gem.

Boat fine, Captain Murphy, and I pilot so sailing be easy for me.

Is this your first time at sea?

Yes, but so what? I pilot, how hard to learn sail small boat...monkey can learn sail!

This is a red rag to a bull and I've had enough of

this bull.

Contract a couple of monkeys then....sure you're a great ape yourself so you'll all get along just dandy!

You are very rude man, why you not want job?

I'm happy to take your boat over but not in this weather. Hurricane Francis is two hundred miles to the east southeast of us and sucking in weather from St. Maarten and beyond...we'd have forty, fifty knots of wind on the nose and a beamy old flat-bottom pig, like a Beneteau 44, ain't designed to weather those sorts of conditions. That's bad enough and now I have to tackle it with one crew who's never been to sea before? Forget it, Igor! You'll have to wait 'til it blows over."

You are scared of little storm?

This simian gobshite is starting to get on my tits. I wonder who's told him to ask me. Geneka cafe is filling up with the other men who work in Nanny Cay and I can hear them cackling at the bar. Stick, Martin, Kevin and Olaf are necking down the beers and hanging on every word of our exchange; mustn't lose face.

I'm not scared of a bit of weather and I've sailed

through plenty but I'm not taking your Tupperware box out in this and that's an end to it big boy.

If you won't then how will I get there?

I think carefully before answering.

Well, you could stick a pelican up your arse and fly there.

What?

You could stick a pelican , I point at one diving into the turquoise waters by the mangroves,
Into your arrogant arsehole,
I lean back in my boson's chair and indicate my own with a considerate forefinger,
And fly there!

I snigger again and make wide and lazy flapping motions with my arms as I lean back from the mast.

There is a howl of laughter from the bar, Devon, the barman, is in hysterics and his high-pitched, abandoned way of laughing, as only West Indian men can, has infected us all. The general mood of mirth has not improved the attitude of my ape.

Maybe I will stick pelican in your arse, Captain

66

Murphy!

Maybe my mate Melbourne at the marine police will sling you in Roadtown jail for a night or two. You'd enjoy that, you can get your prostate checked for free but don't be surprised if the quack doing the checking has both hands on your shoulders and a bit of Barry White on the C.D. player...How d'ya fancy them apples, you big, feckin' gorilla gram?

The laughter at the bar intensifies and my foe's bald pate has turned a livid puce. I may have to remain aloft a while longer than I anticipated. This Cro-Magnon man could make mincemeat of me in a heartbeat.

He is silent awhile and I suddenly feel sorry for him.

I tell you what, I'll bring her over for you next week when the weather's cleared, how's that?

I must leave tomorrow; I am meeting girlfriend on Saturday. I will pay four hundred dollars.

This is getting tempting. I could use the money, that's for sure, the rent is due and I'm all but broke again. I know in my heart it would be madness to venture out in such weather... but its only ninety sea miles and it isn't as though I haven't tackled heavy weather before.

Six hundred, I shout before I know what I'm doing, *Cash only, clear your boat with customs and see Chandi in the office about a contract; I don't want any bullshit if you're a damn smuggler!*

Okay good, very good, anything else I can do?
I can't resist one more jibe.

Sure! Call your girlfriend and tell her to shave her back!

Even he sees the funny side and there it is, the wheels of misfortune are set in motion and Neptune stirs in the depths and sharpens the prongs of his trident...

The British Virgin Islands lie sixty nautical miles to the east of Puerto Rico. They were named by Columbus after St. Ursula and her eleven thousand martyred virgins. For many years they were a refuge for buccaneers who would sell their smoked beef to the Spanish ships that sailed down through the Francis Drake channel on their way to their garrisons in Hispaniola, Jamaica, Cuba and the Spanish Main. These buccaneers would rob the stragglers in the flotilla.

The B.V.I. comprises sixty or so islands and cays of which Tortola is the largest and most populated. It is twelve miles long by three miles wide at the centre. Her steep, vertiginous slopes are covered with lush rainforests and banana plantations, home to millions of tiny tree frogs, whose cacophony of song makes the jungle come alive in an instant as darkness falls as it does so quickly in these latitudes.

Nanny Cay lies off Tortola's southern shore between Road Town (the capital) and West End where I live with my wife and small son. It is separated from the main island by a stone's throw of mangroves and the pretty, green brine. The Cay is half a mile long by a few hundred yards wide. It has a hotel, a marina and three beach bars. North South Yacht Vacations have their offices and workshops at the centre of the main quay. I am a charter captain for them most of the year round and a rigger during hurricane season between June and November.

I finish the job at the masthead and call down to Boots to lower me down to the deck on the winch. He sucks in through his teeth, a West Indian display of disapproval or annoyance.

B'woy, ya crazy goin' out in this weather, ya goin' drown for sure!

He grins wickedly at me.

That's alright, Boots, your Mammy says I can borrow your armbands!

He laughs as we make our way to the office.

When ya boat disappear man, I gonna get private swimming lesson from ya woman, she fine lady!

We get to the office where Chandi is waiting with my contract and pay. I sign the contract and pocket the six hundred and make my way over to Mulligan's for a beer. I am committed now and feel calm. Little do I realise the folly of my decision. I reach Mulligan's shack on the beach by the tiny bridge to Tortola. I pause and gaze south towards Ginger Island. A line squall gallops over the waves towards me as the dark and massing cumulus clouds race overhead. A cold shiver runs up my spine and I hurry to the huddle of friends at the bar, shaking off the sense of foreboding that suddenly overwhelms me.

James gives me a bottle of Red Stripe and is at pains to tell me I've made a poor decision. He is a grizzled Canadian with a reputation for being quick with his fists. He runs a clapped out boatyard at West End where you can get a cheap haul out for a smaller boat with his ancient crane. He has a good heart and we get on well but he is not a man to get on the wrong side of.

Francis is heading north and west but there's another front behind it, not too big but you'll be pushing your luck to leave tomorrow. I hear this guy's never been to sea before so you'll be tackling a rough trip single-handed; you really up to that, Silas? You got your wife and kid to think about...is it really worth it?

I know he's right but there's no way I can borrow the money I need and if I don't make the rent, I'll have to move onto one of Chandi's yachts and give up our lovely apartment in the jungle which won't improve the mood of my wife, who is rarely happy for long these days.

I know you're right, James, and thanks for your concern but I need to do this. They forecast gale force seven tomorrow and the sea state moderate to rough. The wind will be from the Southeast so we'll go over close-hauled and I'll hove to if things get ugly. I'll lose our place on Spyglass Hill if I don't make the rent and Sophia and I have had some problems since Dylan was born. I'm trying to keep her happy if you see what I mean.

He fixes me with a baleful glare. He really is a fierce looking devil.

If she was worth a damn, Murphy, she'd never let you go. Why do you stick your neck out so much for someone who couldn't give a shit? I've never once seen her on the dock with Dylan when your boat comes in and when you're at sea she's too damn friendly with those who ain't!

He spits on the beach to mark his point and leans in closer.

You're a good guy, Silas, little rough round the edges but you need to be round here. But don't be a patsy, no reason Sophia couldn't do a little work round here. There's plenty of work to be had cleaning the yachts when they come in off charter, you know that. Dylan could go in the kindergarten and make some friends. You can't do it all on your own, she should pull her weight a bit more.

We here on my work permit, James, she's not allowed to work. Besides what's the point in having kids if you're gonna pack 'em off to kindergarten? She'd do some work if she could but she ain't allowed so I have to do this and that's that!

The other men at the bar fall silent and I realise they have heard every word we've said. My face burns with shame. Stick, Martin, Kevin and Olaf draw closer to me and James, and order some rum from Mulligan, they hand me one. We put our glasses together and toast.

To the ships on the sea and the ladies on the land, let the first be well-rigged and the second well-manned!

We down our rum in one and slam our shot glasses upside down on the bar in unison. The heat of the rum gives me that warm kiss as it goes down and I feel myself lifted onto that happy plane where I leave my sorrows behind. I am amongst my own kind where I belong, with the dark noisy jungle at my back and the waves hurling themselves at the shore beside our tiny rum-shack. The clouds burst above us, the heavy tropical downpour drumming on the shack's tin roof with a savage, relentless fury. Down on the foreshore, a dog howls at the rain.

I awake with a start at dawn the next day. The jungle is quiet and Sophia and Dylan are sleeping peacefully beside me under the mosquito net. I kiss my boy gently on his forehead and he smiles in his sleep. I slip silently out of our bedroom and into the lounge where I've made up my sea bag the night before.

 I check I've packed my oilskins and sea boots. I put my skipper's license and passport into the oilskin inside pocket. There is my knife and my lifejackets.

I add my dividers and trusty old Portland plotter and last of all a bottle of Cruzan, cheap dark rum, for emergencies.

I stamp on a little yellow scorpion on my way out and make my way down the rough track through the jungle to the main road where James has agreed to pick me up at six.

The road follows the foreshore all the way so I smoke a cigarette on the edge by the shore while I wait. The sky has cleared and the wind subsided over night. Now it's blowing twenty knots or so and the sea state has calmed considerably. I feel reassured and ready for the passage ahead. I hear the putt putting of James' ancient truck behind me and stand up. He leans on the horn and grinds to a halt beside me.

Hey Silas, you goin' ahead with this trip?

Reckon so, I say climbing up into the cab, *Bit calmer now, it should be okay.*

I'll drop you by Nanny Cay, I got to go to Road Town, the crane's hydraulics are blown...wanna help me fix her up when you get back? Twenty bucks an hour okay?

No sweat, I'll swing by day after tomorrow if all

goes well with the trip.

Ten minutes later I'm outside Nanny Cay with my gear and making my way to the visitor's pontoon. I spot the boat immediately. She's a typical ex-charter yacht, posh below deck and weak and poorly rigged above. I check the bottle screws and chain plates for cracks...it is these that take the tremendous pressures on the stays and cap shrouds that support the mast. It wouldn't do to lose the mast. I also check the furling gear for the Genoa and the winches and jack stays. Everything is old and worn but nothing too bad. I check the fuel tanks are full and then stop as the enormous Polish man strides purposefully towards me along the pontoon. He offers his hand and I look him in the eye and shake it.

I'm Silas.

Libor Tyminyetsky. What time we go?

He's an eager beaver and I suppress the urge to laugh.

We've got some checks to do; I need to see your clearance papers and then I've got some jobs for you to do. First up...are you on any medication?

No, I fit...I pilot!

What sort of pilot?

Fighter pilot!

Jesus, Mary and Joseph! How do they get you into the cockpit, with a shoehorn?

It true I big for fighter pilot but I manage, is tight!

I'm starting to warm to this guy. I tell him to stow away everything that's loose below deck while I check the engine over. I plot a course for Philipsburg on the south coast of St. Martin, and then go up to the office to check the latest weather report. It is poor but not horrendous. Last of all we haul out his dinghy and I lash it to the coach-roof abaft the mast. There is no life-raft, I notice, so the dinghy will have to suffice should the shit hit the fan.

 I start the engine and call to Libor below to come on deck. He hauls his ungainly mass up the companion way and grins happily at me. I make a slip with the stern spring and tell him to release the other mooring warps and stow them in the lazarette. I motor back on the stern spring which brings the bow out into the main channel away from the yacht in front of us, and then pop the engine into forward with some revs and away we steam into the channel.

Five minutes later we clear the last of the channel marker buoys and I give the helm to Libor so I can go forward to raise the mainsail.

Keep the bow into the wind, I tell him while I release the mainsheet so the boom is free to swing. I point up at the wind indicator at the mast head; *if you're not sure where the wind is coming from, look at that arrow...it will point towards the direction the wind's coming from. This is the mainsheet and it controls the boom...see these teeth, we call them jammers, when I tell you, you pull the main sheet up into these jammers and that will stop the boom swinging out once we've got the sail up and bear away onto our tack, got it?*

He looks a little bewildered, like a Mormon at a rock festival.

Keep the front of the boat pointing at Ginger Island over there and I'll take care of the rest, ok?

He looks relieved and smiles nervously at me and nods. I go forward and fix the main halyard to the head cringle and haul away quickly. The first set of reef points appear along the sail as it is just over half way up. I lash them in tight with extra line, we'll definitely want all three reefs in for now, and I grab the winch handle and tighten up the halyard so the sail shape is flat and perfect.

I look up to check everything's in order and then scramble back to the cockpit where I make fast the mainsheet so I can bear away when I'm ready. The wind backs into the East so I leave the Genoa furled up and steam directly into the wind to clear Ginger Island.

It's blowing a steady 35 Knots and beyond Ginger Island the seaway is visibly larger than here in the relatively sheltered Francis Drake Channel.

I tell Libor to get his oilskins on and pass mine up. I lend him my spare lifejacket and lifeline so he can clip onto the jackstays for safety when on deck. I suggest he makes up some sandwiches and a flask of soup as I know he won't want to be messing around in the galley once we hit the open sea beyond the channel.

It takes forty minutes to clear Ginger Island and the little yacht starts to pitch violently as she ploughs into the head sea beyond. The wind moans as she blows over the straining steel stays and shrouds, and the bows shudder as they crash into the waves. Every so often she buries her head completely and the seas sweep over the deck and into the coach-roof where they disintegrate into a cloud of spray. It is not long before my eyes are stinging from the salt and I blink away the pain and keep a wary eye out for beam combers.

The rhythm of the sea can lull you into a semi-conscious state where you cope with the job you're doing on autopilot. The wind is on the nose, the seaway's on the nose, then BANG, when you least expect it, and with no rhyme or reason, a great beam sea will break over the side of you and catch you napping.

The various books and manuals about sailing in heavy weather make the assumption that waves come from the same direction as the wind. This is true, generally speaking, but not always. It is important that the bow should be into a large seaway or if you're running before the wind that the seaway is on one or other of the stern quarters of the yacht. The most important point is that it is very dangerous to present the side or beam of the boat to a breaking wave. This can result in a knockdown or worse, a roll. A roll will often dismast the boat and the fallen rig will smash the boat to pieces; then you're in a proper pickle.

Libor is beginning to look unwell. His face has taken a greenish tinge and though he's dry huddled as he is in the shelter of the spray-hood that covers the companionway, I can see that he is sweating.

Come and take the helm for a bit, I tell him, *it'll take your mind off how you're feeling.*

He says nothing and staggers aft to the wheel and sits down next to me. His breathing is short and ragged and I see fear in his eyes. I show him the compass on the binnacle in front of the wheel and tell him to steer 090 or near as dammit. Nobody can manage to steer a boat in these conditions better than five degrees either side of the compass course, but it will keep him busy and that will stop his mind from fretting about his predicament. He starts to look a little better so I tell him to keep a good lookout as I go below for a cup of tea and to mark our position on the chart.

It is noon and we've covered twenty sea-miles so we've averaged five knots. Another seventy miles to Philipsburg so fourteen hours or so before we get in but that's if we get in....the wind and sea-state are building. The noise is overwhelming, the anemometer shows forty five knots of wind and the moan through the rigging has become a constant shrill scream that wears on my nerves.

There is very little fetch, the distance between the waves, and the hull is taking a hiding as she smashes her way through the breaking waves. We will be lucky to maintain five knots in this. I light a cigarette and consider turning back but I realise I've left it too late. There's not enough room between the waves to turn the boat round safely and even if I could, the risk of a broach would be too great and a broach in these conditions would mean death. We're trapped. I finish my tea and fix a cup for Libor and climb up the companionway to join him.

He takes the tea gratefully and shelters under the spray-hood. I take the helm and adjust the course back into the East and squint ahead into the gloom. Visibility is getting poorer by the minute and ahead the sky is as black as sin. I swallow the panic that surges up from the pit of my belly and set my mind to concentrate on the job at hand.

Libor suddenly lurches towards the leeward side of the cockpit and vomits into the gunwales. He pukes and pukes for ten minutes or so until he is left spent, gripping the coaming and dry retching and groaning. I let him stay as he is and manage to give him a pat on the back for encouragement but he's got that thousand yard stare that newcomers so often develop during their first gale and I know it's time to get him below decks and into a bunk on his back. I lash the wheel and quickly help him below decks. I'm staggered to notice he's weeping. I tell him not to worry and help him out of his oilskins and into the starboard coffin bunk. I tell him to lie on his back and think happy thoughts and pull up the bunk's lee-cloth so he doesn't get tipped out when the seaway worsens as I know it will. I put a bottle of mineral water and a bucket on his bunk.

Little sips only. I tell him. Then I wearily climb the companionway to face the trouble ahead. Once I'm back in the cockpit I clip on to the jackstay and sit once more behind the wheel.

I hear the wave before I see it. I struggle frantically with the lashings to free the helm but I know I'm too late and fear grips my innards like a snake. The wave roars like an express train and rears up out of the gloom off the port beam. The lashing comes free and I throw the wheel over to port and slam on some revs to the engine but the wave breaks over us and I'm thrown violently to starboard and all is mercifully silent as I'm submerged completely by the deluge. It seems like an age I'm under and time seems to have stopped then the boat rights herself and shrugs off the sea and back comes the howling noise of the storm.

The engine has stopped and I dare not go below to see why. I quickly make the Genoa's furling line to the secondary winch on the port rail and carefully haul out a third of the headsail with the leeward sheet on the primary winch. Once I'm happy I make fast the furling line and tighten up on the sheet. The yacht starts to make way on a port tack but the best I can pinch to windward is a South-Easterly heading which will add hours to our passage. My heart sinks and I realise I'm hurt as the blood from a cut in my head streams into my eyes and mouth. I pull a bandana out of my oilskin pocket and tie it tightly around my head. The bleeding stops.

There is no sign of Libor and I risk a quick peek below to check he's alright. He is prone on the bunk on his back and silent as a ghost. But I realise now why the engine crapped out as there is a foot of water sloshing around the cabin sole.

I race back to the wheel and open the port locker. I grab the bilge pump handle and work it back and forth with my left hand while I steer the yacht with my right watching and listening carefully for the next rascal to come looming up at us out of the fury of the sea. It takes ages before the bilges are empty and the boat starts to sail better as a result but I am tired and hungry now and the conditions continue to worsen.

 I decide to heave to for a while so I can give myself and the little boat a break. I gently spin the wheel to port and turn her bow through the eye of the wind. Her headsail backs as I leave it made up on the same jib sheet. In effect the main is driving the yacht forward and the headsail's driving her back. This slows the progress through the water and creates drift which flattens the seas before they hit us. The terrible beating through the waves ceases and life becomes bearable though not exactly comfy.

I spin the helm back over so the rudder matches the set of the jib and lash it so the boat can stay hove to. I trim the sails a little so she's balanced and go below. After plotting our position on the chart I gobble down the now soggy sandwiches that Libor made earlier. He is out for the count. We are just over halfway now and I drink some sugary tea and go back on deck where I sit in the shelter of the spray-hood and relax for an hour as the boat lies idle in the gale pitching and tossing but going nowhere.

The fear subsides and gradually I feel my strength returning. I light a cigarette and huddle under the spray-hood which is a little bent out of shape after the hiding we've endured. My thoughts return to Sophia and Dylan and I wonder how they're doing. Sophia will be worried if she's gone to Nanny Cay and they've told her about this weather we're in. I hope she's stayed at home. I spend a little time below trying to get the engine started but the batteries are soaked through I think, and its futile to keep trying.

After a couple of hours the conditions start to improve and the wind speed drops to a steady thirty knots. The seaway softens to a moderate state and I reckon it's time to get cracking.

I unlash the wheel and pay out the working jib sheet so the headsail stops powering us back. As she flogs, I bear away under mainsail then quickly tack and make the jib back up as before on a port tack.

Every hour or so I tack onto a starboard tack to make up for the South Easterly direction we are making. Gradually my confidence returns as we draw closer to the safety of St. Martin's lee shore.

By dawn the following day conditions and visibility have improved and we make landfall at 0720. My relief is almost tangible and even Libor comes on deck looking a little more human.

Still reckon a monkey could learn how to sail, Libor? I give him a wicked grin.

He smiles weakly at me and we sit and chatter happily as the clouds lift and the sun shines down, warming our aching bones. I'm shattered and cannot wait to get in. We have no engine so sail into Philipsburg under the mainsail only. I drop the hook in two fathoms of water and pay out eight fathoms of chain so the anchor has plenty of scope to dig into the sand. I back the mainsail a little to help the anchor dig in and then lower the sail into her stack-pack and go below for a well-earned shot of rum. The aches and pains begin to subside and we go up on deck and unlash the dinghy and put her over the side. We struggle with the outboard as it's still quite choppy even in the shelter of the bay. Ten minutes later we're ashore and after checking in with the astonished customs men we shake hands and part company.

Now I'm ashore I feel weak and giddy. The ground feels as though it is moving because I've been on that pitching deck so long. I settle down on the beach and drink a bottle of Red Stripe.

The air around me suddenly freezes and an invisible weight pins me to the sand. I cannot breathe. I am unable to scream. The periphery of my vision darkens and I see as if through a tunnel. The jumby holds me thus for enough time for me to get his message loud and clear. Then I am released and suck the sweet air into my bursting lungs. I know for sure now that my days at sea are numbered. I am a marked man.

WHEN DADDY CAME ASHORE

Where's Daddy?

I'd rushed through to Mammy's cabin the minute I'd woken up, so. I couldn't wait to see him. He'd been away at sea for six weeks. I was so excited. Couldn't contain it!

What's the matter with you, Dylan? He's at sea, boy. You know that. He'll be home next week.

He's back already, Mammy! I saw him, so!

I couldn't believe her stupidity. Imagine Daddy getting in and Mammy not knowing? Is she thick so?

He's home, I tell you! He woke me up in the night! We talked and talked. He was wet, Mammy! Sure maybe he's gone shopping. P'raps he's on deck!

Well, he didn't wake me, are you sure?

I'm sure, Mammy, let's find Daddy now, come on!
I scrambled up the companion way. Big steps. Mammy hot on my heels.

Deck was deserted, though.

He's probably gone to Roadtown. Bet he's gone to get presents. He always brings you a dress and me a toy, doesn't he Mam?

He does Dylan but I don't think he's back. You probably dreamt it.

I didn't dream it he was dripping all over me, must have been a squall. And I told you, he woke me up and we were talking. He told me a funny story. He'll be in Roadtown, you wait and see.

We went back below and Mammy fixed breakfast. I wasn't hungry, though. Too excited. By lunchtime he still wasn't back.

Sure he'll be at Nanny Cay; I bet he's doing some rigging for Chandi. Let's go to nanny Cay, Ma, we'll find him there I know it!

Well if he's not home at least you can have a swim at the pool. Are you sure he was there and you didn't just dream it, Dylan.

I didn't dream it, Mammy. I saw him, how many times do I have to tell you. Come on let's go to Nanny Cay; we can take the RIB.

Alright, put your lifejacket on. Do I look okay?

You look lovely, Mam, come on!

Be patient, Dylan, I want to put some lipstick on. I want to look nice for your Dad.

I'll have a long white beard by the time you're ready, come on!

Eventually she was ready and we set off for Nanny Cay. It was a beautiful day, the heat tempered by the soft trade winds. The turquoise sea illuminated by the Caribbean sun. I felt as if our Rib was suspended in a blue forever. We raced over the gentle swells and got to Nanny Cay in no time. It was busy. Charter boats coming and going. Men climbing the rigs to fix stuff. It was the perfect childhood, you know.

I saw Harry under the awning outside the charter company's workshop. He was trying to splice loops into mooring warps. He was making a hash of it. Daddy would laugh when he saw this, for sure. I ran over to talk.

Hey, Harry, those are terrible splices you're laying in there! Have you seen my Dad?

What do you mean? Cheeky hooligan! Your Dad's not due back for a couple of days yet. He'd have had a bit of weather to cope with. How did you and your Mum enjoy your stay on my boat last night?

Oh we loved it, Harry! Mammy says we're going to give up our place in the jungle and live on a boat for always. She doesn't like the snakes! She doesn't like the big walk. When we're on the boat we can get everywhere in the dinghy. It's fun I love living on the boat. I'm going to be a captain like you and Daddy when I'm a big boy! You're wrong about Daddy, though, he woke me up last night but we can't find him. He must be in Roadtown buying presents, probably.

Oh, he must have made it to St. Maarten quicker than I thought he would. I'm glad you liked staying on Fairwind, tell your Mummy you can stay on her as long as you like but your Dad needs to do some work on the engine and the rig for me in exchange. You tell him I want to see him when you find him, okay?

Okay, Harry. You'd be better cutting out those terrible splices and just tie bowlines instead. Daddy will take the piss out of you for sure when he sees those; you know what he's like.

Harry grinned wolfishly and pinched my nose and told me to bugger off. Mammy laughed.

We stayed at Nanny Cay the whole day and I swam

in the pool with my friends. I'm a good swimmer and stopped needing armbands when I was one and a half. Now I'm four and a half. Everybody says I look like my Dad. My Dad is big and very funny. Sometimes he has a beard when he comes ashore and Mammy won't let him kiss her 'til he shaves it off. She squeals when he tries.

Daddy never came back that day or the next.

I was very sad for a while and Mammy was quiet and got cross with me quite a lot.

Two days later Daddy came onboard Fairwind very late in the night. I woke up and went into the cabin.

We laughed and joked and he told me all about his voyage. He was in a big storm called Hurricane Francis. The boat he was in charge of nearly sank. I asked him how he was able to come and see me in the night the other day at the same time he was in the storm.

He told me he was thinking about me and Mam in the worst of the weather. He said when we are facing difficult times our souls can travel on the wind and visit the people we love. Mammy doesn't want him to go to sea anymore. Neither do I.

JUMBY BOAT

She awoke me at two that morning. The jungle was alive. A cacophony of tree frogs. It was a new moon and the trades were blowing a steady twenty knots. I knew this from the sound of the breakers down on the foreshore. There'd be quite a seaway running through the passage at Green Cay.

I dressed quickly and put the clasp knife in my right pocket. The sheath knife was on my belt in the small of my back. They both had a keen edge. We'd haul the gear at Whalebank today. It had soaked for a week.

I wolfed down the coffee and kissed her. She was warm and voluptuous. I didn't want to go to sea. I wanted to go back to bed and fuck her.

I made my way down to the foreshore through the jungle. I disturbed a snake on the way. He fled into the dense foliage. Strange shadows danced around me as the clouds drifted over the moon.

The outboard started on the third pull. I'd replaced the spark plug yesterday. I steered the little whaler out to the western headland and made my way round the point to Great Harbour. What little moon there was would be gone in half an hour.

I stood out to sea to avoid the worst of the combers breaking close in to the point. A fin broke the surface off to starboard. Black tip.

It was calmer at Great Harbour. I tied up behind Ocean Jem and lit a cigarette. Foxy was walking down the jetty with a bushel of bananas. Manny was drinking a Guinness in the wheelhouse. I went on board with a heavy heart. I pushed the drum of cowhides to the stern. The stench of death was overwhelming.

We put out to sea at three. The men stood talking quietly on the afterdeck as we made way into the darkness. The seaway at Green Cay picked up the bow and threw us into the trough. Short seas. The waves crashed into the wheelhouse. Visibility was zero and I made my way through the tiny gap in the reef by instruments only. I adjusted to starboard to allow for the fierce cross current and the set of the breakers. After all this time it still made me sweat. I sang "Roadhouse Blues" under my breath.

Well I woke up this morning, and I got myself a beer,
The future's uncertain, and the end is always near...

We cleared the reef at three thirty and I set the autopilot northwest for Whalebank. We'd get there at dawn. Only twelve strings to haul and set. The men came in and Foxy sat at the wheel, Manny on the bench abaft it. I went aft for a cigarette and to drink the coffee she'd made me earlier. The moon had gone now. I was alone in the darkness.

At first I thought it was a cruise ship. It was too close for that. It was just a glow off the port bow. I threw the cigarette away and stared into the gloom. The boat took form slowly at first. It was a cutter. Gaff rigged with two headsails. She carried no running lights. I wondered why. I didn't realise her close proximity to us until I saw the phosphorescence in the bow wave. In that moment I knew we were going to collide.

I swallowed the panic and ran through to the wheelhouse. The men too had seen her. I glanced out of the port window to check. She was half a cable away and closing fast. I shut off the auto helm and swung the wheel violently to starboard and gave the engine some thrust. It wouldn't stop the inevitable collision. It would mean we'd take it on the port lazarette. There was a watertight bulkhead there. At least we wouldn't sink. This was no place to go swimming. Sharky.

I looked up again to check the collision was as I wanted it. The boat had vanished.

The men's faces had a tinge of green. They were black normally.

For a while the silence was deafening.

Manny broke it.

We ain't goin' to Whalebank, Captain.

I knew their strength and hadn't the minerals to argue. I marked down the Lat/Long co-ordinates in the log-book and wrote ANOMALY beside them. Then we headed in. Nobody spoke.

Manny dropped the hook in two fathoms and I set the stern against the jetty as usual. Foxy tied us off to the cleats. The men left immediately so I hosed down the boat on my own. I changed the fine fuel filter and cleaned out the Racal. Then I went back into the wheelhouse to switch off the radio. We always monitor channel 16. The emergency channel.

It crackled to life.

Mayday, mayday, mayday, this is Dive boat Sally Anne, mayday. We have a diver down, mayday this is Sally Anne.

They called out their Lat/Long position and I marked it down in my log-book and switched on the engine. Then I waited for the response from the coastguard. They dispatched a chopper within five minutes so I cut the engine and waited.

Seven of them had been diving and one had gone missing. Good visibility and slight seaway as the tide was at the stand.

A cloying sense of dread overwhelmed me. The hair stood up on the back of my neck. The blood drained from my head. I turned over the page of my log-book with hands that were shaking.

The co-ordinates were the same as our anomaly that morning.

They found his remains on Boxing Day. Part of his torso. Still in his stab-jacket. The sharks'd had the rest.

RIPTIDE

I'd listened to her in silence. I was too stunned to respond verbally. My responses were physical but not so much that she'd have noticed them. She used clichés, of course, which might have irritated me had I not been rendered dumb by the enormity of her message.

We need to talk...

I took it all in from a dizzy perspective. I didn't comprehend immediately, I think. Shock plays tricks on the mind.

I've met someone...

My happy family had been an illusion. Change is swift and cold. It shatters the illusion. Our hopes and dreams become so much flotsam and jetsam on the high water mark. And we, when it happens, are useless, empty shells beside them, scoured clean and discarded by an indifferent sea.

I love you but I'm not in love with you...

Nausea and panic collided and I broke into a cold sweat. She didn't notice. She was immersed completely in her carefully prepared monologue.

It's not you, it's me...

The whole day had been an illusion. We had made love when we awoke that morning. We'd risen, taken the children to lunch in Exeter and gone shopping. We had laughed, told jokes, bought the children some new clothes and some new toys. We had bought her some new clothes too. I was engulfed by a wave of nausea as I remembered this.

I can't help the way I feel...

She'd linked arms with me and smiled coquettishly as she steered me into the Anne Summers shop. The lingerie she chose was expensive. Not all expense is monetary. I realise that now. The lingerie hadn't been chosen for me. That smile, I wonder about that now. At the time it was a smile from one lover to another. It had been a secret between us, a promise of further intimacy.

I think of you now as a brother...

I thought I knew all her smiles. She had one that was false when she didn't understand the joke. She had one that was real when she did. She had the one that was ours that promised love. Perhaps I'd confused that one with another I hadn't known. The one that mocks. The one that Brutus wore.

I know we'll always be friends...

We'd returned from Exeter, had a light supper and I had put the children to bed while she had a bath before her kickboxing class. Who bathes before exercise? Her class should have finished at nine but she returned at one. She'd gone for drinks with some of the other girls in the class afterwards. They'd had mojitos and danced, they were a great crowd. She went upstairs and had another bath and came down in some of the new lingerie. We made love in front of the fire. It had always been good but never so intense. It was the last time, you see. Only she had known that. Ignorance, bliss, it's all true.

The children will live with you...I need my space...we'll figure out a routine so I can see them often...

We build our lives and with them our illusions. The two are connected as if by a marriage vow. A hollow vow has the same substance. I met her kickboxing coach in the village a few days later. He'd been surprised that she'd missed so many classes, she hadn't been for weeks.

I never meant to hurt you...

I am not yet alcoholic. I am dipsomaniac. I drink on

a full moon when I'm lighter. I drink enough to exist. There is no past and no future when I drink. I drink until I am numb and feel nothing. The alcohol is novocaine for my soul. I choose a night when the children are with their mother.

To have and to hold...

I become an inconsequential part of my surroundings. My brain ceases to function properly. The clock stops. I breathe in and out and my heart pumps the blood around but only because it can. If I'm hungry and I remember, I eat.

For better for worse...

When I awake I am calm and hung-over but the pain has gone and with it my anxiety. The children return and I bury myself in the routine of being a single Dad. I believe in the love between us. They are too young and too pure to have learnt how to fake that.

For richer for poorer...

We have become a family of three. They screamed when I told them mummy had moved out. That image haunts me. They are young to have to suffer such a disappointment. They are also resilient and I am proud of them. I was a sailor and my children understand the moon and the tide. I have taught them that if ever they are caught in a riptide, they must swim across it and never against it.

In sickness and in health...

They are both swimming strongly now. I observe this with relief whilst treading water myself. I am tired and the current is dragging me further and further out to sea. I'd be alright if only I had a little sloop to tack back to shore with.

To love and to cherish...

It's no accident that boats have female names. They require a captain and a crew who must work together like a family. But the boat itself is the centre of that universe. The boat is the matriarch. The boat comes first, the crew second and lastly the captain. Look after the boat and she'll look after you. It is the end if you forget this basic rule.

Til death do us part...

There is not one molecule within us that cannot be found in the sea. We will all become part of it eventually.

HOPE

She was walking down from the square past the baker's. She walked like a little bird. Like a little bird she walked from the Square in Chagford and she walked down the hill. She stopped at the arch that led into the cafe called The Courtyard. Like a beautiful bird she stopped outside The Courtyard. And then she went in.

His instinct was to follow. There was some element of danger to this man. He was dangerous because he was not afraid to follow his instincts. He was not drunk. He had only drunk enough to be numb. He followed his instinct. He followed her into The Courtyard.

It was a small and cosy cafe. They sold organic food and the walls were hung with paintings by local artists. She was inside choosing vegetables. She chose with care.

He went in and picked up a packet of cous cous that he neither wanted nor needed. He stood with his cous cous and he gazed at her.

She had a calm and ethereal aura. She was beautiful, of course. High cheekbones. Piercing, light blue eyes. Long, dark hair. Slender. His instinct was to engage her. He enjoyed following his instincts.

She joined the small queue at the counter and he took his place behind her, the unwanted cous cous clutched in his right hand.

She wouldn't normally talk to a stranger. She was shy. She was shy because as a child she'd had a speech impediment. Her thoughts were deep and plentiful. But she didn't waste words. Like her food she chose them carefully. Normally, at least.

Like a little bird of paradise, she turned her head and looked at him.

He was surprised when she turned around and looked at him. Her pale, cobalt eyes looked straight through him. He wondered if she knew he had followed her.

That's a simple supper you're having tonight. She said to him with a smile. He smiled back at her.

And you too. Is it better to keep life simple? He couldn't take his eyes from hers.

I do lead a simple life and prefer to keep it basic. I try only to buy what I need as I cannot afford more. I need water to drink which is free. I need fruit and vegetables which cost a little. I need paint and some other bits and pieces and these cost more. So these are my needs and they are few as you can see. She smiled again. A shy smile.

He leaned in close to her and whispered conspiratorially into her ear.

I am buying this cous cous here. But it is a lie! I neither want it nor need it. Sure, I don't even know what it is, so! Will you let me buy you a cup of tea?

This time her smile was big and he could see all of her pretty white teeth. She nodded and they paid and ordered and took a tiny table at the window. Outside it was raining. Behind the counter the girls noticed what had happened and smiled at the romance. The truth is not always harsh. It is sometimes kind and fertile. It is sometimes a second chance. It can be renaissance.

So why did you buy the cous cous?

I needed a reason to bump into you!

I knew it! I stopped outside because I had a feeling something strange was happening. I felt dizzy. What's your name?

Silas, what's yours?

Lara. Do you live in the village?

I live a mile outside. Below the Ascot's farm at Great Weeke. It is a very old cottage at the bottom of the hill to starboard. There is a stream in the garden and some broken boats. It is basic but beautiful. I like it as it is away from the press of humanity. I too live a simple life. I live with my two small children. My boy is eight and my daughter seven. Their mother left on Valentine's Day. It has been a hard year for them but they are brave and resilient and I am proud of them.

What is it that you do for your living?

I used to go to sea. I was a contract captain. Yachts and fishing vessels. Now I stay at home as I have had to be a mother as well as a father. We don't have central heating so I fell trees with my friend Julian in Spreyton in exchange for firewood. The rest of the time I write and look after my children. What do you do?

I am an artist. I have a studio in Throwleigh. I paint but I also have to work at the Three Crowns for money. I am a waitress there and sometimes I work behind the bar. My studio is above the Tythe Barn opposite the church in Throwleigh. It is most basic. I have to fill my water bottle at Trevor's house and he will let me shower there. If I need the toilet there is one next to the church. Sometimes I spend the night at my boyfriend's house in Okehampton.

This last sentence struck Silas like a punch in the chest. He was speechless for a moment but then she asked him what he wrote about and her eyes were kind and he relaxed.

I write about the sea and her meanings. Sometimes I write other stuff but keep the sea in the background as a metaphor.

A metaphor for what? She asked him.

The human condition. I think that we become existential after some time at sea. Time ceases to have any meaning. The past is irrelevant and the future uncertain. We live in a long and seemingly endless moment with Death watching our every move from the shadows. He comes quickly and is impartial. We exist in a hostile environment that cares not if we live or die. We eat and drink and we struggle. We hope to make landfall and get in safely. But after a while it doesn't seem to matter. What do you paint?

He was elated to be sitting opposite this beautiful girl. He was confused, however.

On the one hand she seemed to be interested in him. But she had wasted little time letting him know she had a boyfriend. If this boyfriend was so special, why was she sitting here having tea with him? A complete stranger. Why was she showing such a transparent interest in him? Why?

These were his thoughts as Lara sat quietly, sipping her tea and contemplating his question. What do you paint? Her eyes never left his for a moment. She saw the sea in his eyes and something else. Not fear but something like danger or the knowledge of it. Death itself, perhaps? She found him compelling.

She never met new people with Desmond. He was dyslexic and unable to read. He preferred to watch T.V. He was a good man and kind but she had known for some time that she was with him because she felt an obligation to him.

Desmond did not understand her work anymore than he understood her. They were disconnected. He had few ideas of his own. This was not his fault. It was simply due to the fact that he was unable to read and so didn't. His knowledge, therefore, was limited. If she had an idea and expressed her thoughts on it to him, he would regurgitate her ideas when questioned on that subject by a third party. He had nothing fresh of his own to add as his intellect and comprehension were stunted by his lack of knowledge. He had no wish to correct this and filled the vacuum with violent movies instead. At length she answered his question.

I paint landscapes and still life. When I have an idea I paint themes and metaphors. I rarely paint portraits. Portraits are lucrative, it's true, but I do not paint for silver. I paint what I see but it's hard as my perspective alters as the idea deepens and assumes a life of its own. I will sometimes paint a portrait but only when I feel it. Only when I want to. When I choose to.

Would you paint a portrait of the Queen if she asked you to? Silas asked her with a mischievous grin.

No, I don't know her. I might if I knew her and grew to love her from knowing her. But not for her silver. Not like that. Never.

I'd be interested to come and see your work if you'd allow it?

And I will, Silas, but you must let me read yours!

They smiled at each other in silence for a moment. And then they swapped numbers. And then she left.

Silas watched her leave and then walked back to the Square where he'd left his car and gundog, Finian. He drove directly to Sandy Park and parked his car at the Inn. He walked across the road to Patrick's house.

The drive down to Sandy Park only takes a few minutes but it's a beautiful drive. Over the river at Rushford and rolling pasture all the way. The little journey always soothed his turbulent mood. It would be many long years before he could return to the sea to which he was so impossibly addicted and it was this most lovely part of Devon that was the only place he wanted to be for those years.

He didn't knock on Patrick's door but went straight in. He went into the small kitchen and filled the kettle and put in on. Then he called up the stairs.

Come down, Paddy. I've had a strange morning!

As Patrick came stomping down the stairs, Silas wondered how much longer the Stena stair lift would remain in its redundant place on the first flight that had led to Dion's room.

Hello, Silas! Good timing, I've had enough. Let's go to the pub. I want one of their cappuccinos! Brain's fried and I'm suffering from cabin fever!

How's the book coming?

Not going to talk about it today. But I've started and I'm excited about it. Come on, I need a coffee.

Silas left the cups and they walked over the road to the Inn. Shona was behind the bar on the phone and smiled at them as they went in. They sat at the fireside and waited patiently. The pub was empty. Shona finished taking the booking and greeted the men with a friendly smile.

Hey Paddy, hey Captain! Pint of Otter?

Cappuccino for me, please. Said Patrick.

I'll have a pint. Silas grinned. *How's Goaty?*

He's at home with the boys and they're all fine. He's probably trying to practise and Gulliver and Erivan are probably stopping him with their mischief. He has a gig in Exeter on Thursday. Are you going?

Aye, we'll be there, so!

Yes, I could just do with a night out.

There are no coincidences. Just serendipity and

synchronicity. Signposts and omens. Silas had returned from the West Indies five years earlier with Sophia and their two small children, Dylan and Claire. Ten months ago she had left them for horses and land and the comfort of relative wealth and mediocrity.

Goaty had returned from his own adventures at sea four years earlier and had met Shona and fallen head over heels in love. She had rescued him from the claws of the sea's vice-like grip on his heart and they had taken over the Sandy Park Inn with his parents as the new Landlords.

It was the only place Silas felt comfortable in his new incarnation as a landsman. It was the only place he felt comfortable enough to drink in. It was the place he could be drunk and in his cups and they were good enough and liked him enough to understand and leave him alone.

Before that, they hadn't seen each other since they'd fitted out Beansidhe together all those years ago.

No kids tonight? Patrick asked Silas.

Nah, they're with their Mammy tonight.

Tell me about this strange morning then.

I saw a beautiful woman this morning, Paddy. Well, a girl, really. In the Square, so. And I followed her, Paddy.

You're a stalker, Silas!

I am so! And I followed her into the Courtyard. And Ella was behind the counter with Jess. And I bought some feckin cous cous. And the girls saw through me and they tried not to laugh.

Why did you buy cous cous?

I wanted to talk to the girl.

Who is she?

An artist.

Where from?

Throwleigh. Above the Tythe Barn.

Well? What happened?

She spoke to me. We drank tea together. She has a boyfriend.

Ah. A boyfriend. Life can never be simple, Silas, can it?

On the contrary, Paddy, Our very first conversation was about the simplicity of our lives.

Silas explained the meeting in detail to his friend and paraphrased the conversation as well as he could remember. When he'd finished they drank their beers in companionable silence and returned to the bar for a refill. By this time the bar had filled up. Shona had gone to the kitchen and Andrea had taken over serving at the bar. Chris walked in with his young spaniel, Milly, who lay down with her friend Finian at the fireside. The three men stood quietly at the bar awaiting their turn to be served.

Silas has been stalking a young artist from Throwleigh, Patrick said to Chris. *Shall we incarcerate him?*

Ah, that must be young Lara. Chris drawled laconically. *Splendid girl, that! Bloody talented artist indeed. Made a play for her myself. Last year I think. No dice. You ought to go and see her work. Blow your tiny minds.*

I mean to. Silas said. *I'm going to call her tomorrow.*

What are you working on, Paddy? Chris asked.

I don't want to talk about it. Something here.

Bronze Age. A blind king. Anger. First person. Tricky business. Need a drink actually. Ask Silas, bloody words are pouring out of him, smug little fucker! How many stories now, Silas?

Twelve. I'm done. But I have to write the blurb that goes on the back and I'm stuck. How can I be objective about my own work? Anything I have to say about it must be subjective by definition. I can't do it.

Stuck! Chris spat the word. *I've spent six weeks and the better part of five hundred on alcohol on the piece I'm writing now. It's supposed to be cathartic. Alcoholic blackouts. I'm going to email it to you both when I'm done. But tonight I am not going to fall off the wagon. Tonight I am going to hurl myself from it! I want whisky. Anyone else?*

Rum. Silas said quietly.

Otter. Patrick nodded with a grin.

They tucked into their drinks with abandon and Chris asked Silas what he was writing. They often met and traded ideas and although he felt that their ability was far beyond his own, it helped Silas to talk with these remarkable men. Today, however he didn't want to talk about the book he was writing. He'd signed the contract and was excited about it but couldn't concentrate on his work so consumed was he by the thought of Lara. He told Chris that he would email it.

I'm happy to read it but I know I'll hate it so no critique. It will either be dreadful and so I will hate it. Or it will be excellent and better than my own so I will hate it all the more!

Paddy and Silas exchanged looks.

Hemingway! They shouted mockingly in unison.

Didn't think you'd catch that, well done! Chris admitted with an apologetic smile.

I want to talk to you about the meaning of hope. Silas said suddenly. And his face had darkened. He looked fierce. There was a pause as the men thought.

It's a cliché, said Patrick, *like tomorrow's another day.*

Is it an emotion? Asked Silas.

No, said Chris, *it's deeper. More primal. Tied up with evolution, perhaps. We were hunter/gatherers before we evolved towards the idea of animal husbandry, farming and then surplus and thereby wealth. We hoped we'd eat that day. We hoped the fire would start. We hoped we'd survive.*

But that's a conscious thought, Patrick interjected, *not an emotion. Hope is more than the one thing or the other. You are wrong. Hope is connected with faith but real faith rather than the blind variety that is beaten into the dispossessed by the church and those other organisations that seek only to calm and control the weak and the damned.*

Profound but we're not there yet. Chris drawled. *What do you think, Andrea?*

Well, a little bird told me that hope was the last thing to die. She said, pouring out three shots of the Mount Gay rum, which Goaty kept on the shelf for his old mate, and then three pints of beer. *It's your turn to pay, Silas. No sneaking off to the loo in the hope these poor buggers will pick up the bill!*
He paid up with a toothy grin. *Anyway, you posed the question, what do you think hope means?*

The men emptied their rum and had some beer. There was a pause while they waited for Silas to speak. At length he began.

I drink when I don't have the children with me

because up until now I felt that I must. When I went to sea I drank to hide myself and to forget. Now I drink to remember. At sea I was alive but as if in a dream. Death was no stranger to us. He roamed freely amongst us like a companion. We could smell him. And he smells like fear. And he smells like corruption. Hope would scour that stench away. But I did not like hope for I thought he was blind. I thought of hope as a useless cripple and no friend of mine.

I was a selfish man and arrogant. My friendships meant nothing to me. Ashore my attitude to my lovers was the same. If I wanted a thing I would take it and damn the consequences.

Fear was for the greenhorns and I despised them. I lived and breathed. I ate and drank. What was the point in thinking or feeling? I was numb and adrift and I liked it that way.

There were times in heavy weather when one or other of the crew would come to me, "Will we be alright, Silas? Will we get in this time?" I would look scornfully at them and depending on their condition as I perceived it would either double their workload or send them below to their bunks. I had no regard for them. No feeling. Just scorn.

Death held no fear for me. I knew him well. I

couldn't understand why he hadn't already come for me. It seemed unfair. I knew in my heart and what was left of my shattered soul that it was just a matter of time. But he mocked me. He would sneak up and grab the good and the young and the weak and the hopeful.

I was still a boy when I lost my faith and with it my hope.

I have spent ten years sailing fruitlessly around the globe. Those passages were meaningless moments in an environment that cares not who lives or dies. I didn't question it. I simply existed, pointlessly with neither hope nor faith.

But now, today, a sea change has come. It is not a subtle change but a momentous one that has struck me like a hard punch to the point of the jaw! My teeth have been rattled, boys, and with them my soul. I am alive! I am Silas Murphy and I live! You have been my friends for some years yet today I see you with different eyes because a young girl called Lara has opened them for me. Today I feel love for you and when we are drunk and Andrea tells us to leave so she can close the pub we will return to our homes. And I will awake with a blistering headache and still I will love you. And all because I have met this girl. And she will never be mine! She will not be mine because I am old and broken and ugly. But she will be my friend. She will be my friend and despite her boyfriend she may choose to be more. And that, my friends, that is hope.

It was still dark when he awoke the following morning. His head throbbed and he was cold. His dog was pulling off his bedclothes. He wanted to go for a walk. He fed the dog then pulled on his old pea coat and went out into the darkness. Despite the hangover he felt differently to usual. Even the dawn was different today. It was no longer a hollow vow in the East. Today it was a promise. A rosy kiss that suffused Meadowbank with pink and feminine sexuality.

He took his time to recover from the brutality of his hangover. His bones ached but he shrugged off the pain as he would a poorly timed punch. Two magpies flew out from the copse beside him as he walked. Two for joy. And he returned to his cottage. And the sun came up and shone. He spared a thought for Sophia but even those thoughts had changed. She seemed now to him to be little more than a false memory. A disconnected smile in passing. Everything had changed.

He called Lara at ten but it went straight to answer phone.

At eleven it was the same.

At noon she answered.

Silas, she said, *I knew it would be you.*

Hello, Lara, I was, er, hoping to come and see you. I mean not you. Your work. I mean not that. Ah fuck's sake I'm talking shit again. What I'm trying to say, Lara is that I'd like to come and see you and your work!

You're funny, she giggled, *come over, then. I'm at the studio now.* And she hung up.

Silas took a bath. He looked at himself in the mirror. He looked old. He looked rough. A beard had appeared on his weathered face. He wouldn't fight himself. He wouldn't care to meet himself in a dark and anonymous alley. His heart sank. Friends, he thought, friends will be fine. She will be my friend. But maybe...

The drive to Throwleigh took him along all the pretty back lanes. He stopped at the Northmore Arms to murder the remains of his hangover with a little shot of rum and then he drove his battered granny car on to Throwleigh, a tiny cluster of medieval cottages with thatched rooves around an old Norman church. He parked and walked up past the church to the Tythe Barn. He paused outside by the little wooden steps that ran up the gable end. His heart was in his mouth and the door above was a stable door and it opened and she came out.

She had not heard him, despite the silence of her surroundings. But she had known that he was there. His Labrador ran up the steps and stopping only briefly to lick her hand, went into the studio and lay down. Silas followed. He paused at the top of the steps. They looked into each other's eyes and he kissed her lightly on her cheek. She shivered and they followed the dog inside.

The studio was small and it was old. It had great oak purlins supporting the roof. Paintings covered every wall and were stacked in every corner. All the accoutrements of her trade lay in piles everywhere he looked. The atmosphere was heady and the room felt like home.

She said something but he did not hear.

You'll have to speak up a little, he said, *I have all but lost my hearing in the left ear.*

What happened?

I'm deaf in that ear because I did a job for some

wealthy people. They were rich and so did not need to do it themselves. They paid me to do it as they knew I was poor and so would. I salvaged their boat and the water there was very dirty as they knew. It was dirty so I got an infection in my ear. And the infection was in my ear for two years. It would not go. For two years I took medications but still it would not go.

Finally I saw a witch in Tortola and she cured the infection with some fire ants. It was painful but she cured it. By now I was deaf in that ear. And I was deaf because the wealthy had paid me to be so. And I fall down when I am ashore. Sometimes I fall down because I am drunk and sometimes because I am deaf. But when I go to sea I can balance. And my balance at sea is beautiful and remarkable and strange. But only at sea is this true. And I don't like wealthy people. I don't like them because they took my hearing and my balance and they paid me two thousand for it.

Lara was silent for some time and then she made a decision.

I'm going to show you a painting I have done and I want you to tell me what it is that I have painted, ok?

He waited quietly while she pulled out a canvas

from the stack by the door.

It showed a small dark room. A girl was seated at a table, her head and right arm resting on its surface. Her other arm hung lifelessly at her side. She was in total despair. A man was walking out of the door and his shadow fell across her feet as he left.

Silas gazed at the painting for ages. Then he took Lara in his arms and looked into her eyes once more.

You have painted Grief, he said and there were tears welling up in his eyes. *You have painted Grief and he has clearly been your companion for you to be able to capture him so well. He is my companion too and he has worn me out!*

I have finished with my boyfriend this morning, she told him in a low voice. *I am going to need you to stop drinking alcohol, Silas. We are going to take our time and begin as a little more than friends and one day we will be lovers. But for now I want you to stop drinking and forgive yourself and then I can make you happy and you can make me happy.*

He hugged her then with the ferocity of a storm. And the tears flowed down his face. And she kissed him then. It was a kiss that consumed him.

And after the kiss there was hope. Only hope. The world shrank. The clocks stopped. All but the kiss was peripheral and meaningless. They kissed again and when they did, it was only hope that remained. He didn't realise he was crying. All he knew was hope and the certain knowledge she had saved him.

THE LAST VOYAGE

It's for the best, Silas. You'll be happier there. You'll have friends your own age, lovely meals three times a day, activities and your own room. You'll be waited on hand and foot by all those pretty young nurses. You'll be able to tell them all your sea stories. They'll love you!

My niece. Conniving little psycho. She has power of attorney over me. How the fuck did I let that happen? She moved into my house with her snotty husband and now she's moving me out. Her fellow's a lawyer. He's also an M.P. Puny little bastard. Bony girl arms and a supercilious sneer. Sure I'm thinking I might kill him.

Son of a bitch has a 49 foot Hallberg-Rassy on a pontoon on the other side of the river at Kingswear. He never takes her out. Crime that. He calls himself a Day Skipper. Little bollocks. She's worth quarter of a million and lies idle on her pontoon.

His expenses! Sure, he's one of those. A house here, a flat there, the taxpayer picking up his tab. He doesn't think of them as taxpayers, he refers to them as the masses, the hoi polloi.

My house looks over the water. River frontage. Dartmouth. Desirable. They desire it so they take it.

The rich get richer. Carelessness pays. They accumulate their wealth, rolling through life like a faecal tide, leaving a wake of iniquity behind them. Egocentric, thoughtless and focussed always and ever on the plunder. I'm not going to let them win.

You're not putting me in a nursing home.

You'll love it; Goaty's there now. He's your best friend.

He hates it, I'll hate it. I'm not going. This is my home. Why don't you fuck off back to London? I don't need you. I don't want you here! I can look after myself, so!

We can't look after you here. We're just not qualified. You'll be seventy next month. You need professional care. The Cedars will provide that. There's no other option, Silas. You'll see it's for the best. I have to go out now. I'll be back at ten tonight. Simon will be home tomorrow. We'll help you pack then. There's a plate of fish fingers in the fridge. Microwave them for two minutes.

I say nothing. She leaves, slamming the door. I listen to her footsteps as she power walks along the street in her ridiculous high heels. Click clack click clack.

I decide to find out just how much control she has over me. I go to the bank to see if she's gelded me financially. They have no problem with my request to transfer all my funds into an offshore account. There is a small fee. My savings add up to about twenty thousand in dollars. It'll be dollars I need.

I go into my study. Simon has taken it over completely. I spend an hour going through his stuff. Steal what I need!

Then I call Goaty. They won't let me speak to him. Fuckers. I take a taxi to the home and ask the driver to wait down the road.

He's alone in his spartan room. His face lights up when he sees me.

How's yer luck, Silas?

Grand so! Bet you're loving this place. Why didn't they let you speak to me when I phoned?

They're angry. The polish boy was taking the piss, little bastard. I knocked him out!

You're not happy then?

I hate it here!

How long's it been since we went to sea, Goaty?

Jesus, must be twenty years now.

You still fit enough, Boy?

Course! Why?

We're going out for a walk now. You coming?

Fuckin' right.

Will the staff here allow it?

They will. I'm allowed to go for a walk with visitors.

Right so, get your warmest clothes on now, we're leaving! Still got your passport?

I do. We ain't coming back are we, Silas? I'd rather die than return 'ere, Boy!

Be silent, Goaty, we ain't coming back!

We slip silently out of the huge Victorian house and into the winter rain. The taxi is waiting patiently down the road.

Sainsbury's. I tell the driver as we get in, *quick as you like!*

We fill four trolleys and pay. The taxi brings us to the quay. I tip the ferryman a tenner to help us to carry on the victuals.

Five minutes later we are on D pontoon at Kingswear. Sweet Pea lies forlorn and neglected. Goaty goes onboard with the ease and practise of years. Simon has no business possessing such a yacht. We are giggling as we stow the victuals carefully below in the saloon.

You square away the deck and make ready, Silas, I'll check the engine!

Aye, aye, Goaty!

Nobody bothers us. We are invisible. Tide's starting to ebb as we put out to sea. We set sail outside the buoyage. Calm. We reach over to Start Point. She's a beautiful craft and sails herself now we've trimmed the sails just so. Wind backs into the east and strengthens. Seaway starts to build. Goaty's singing the Irish Rover. Salt in our eyes and joy in our hearts. We're back where we belong at last!

We clear the point at twilight and bear away westward on a dead run.

Spain or the West Indies, Goaty?

Antigua first, then the Butterfly, I reckon I know where there's gold!

We have a nip of rum to stay the cold and run ever westward into the night.

Dominic Morgan was born at his grandmother's house in Instow, North Devon. Where her garden ended, the beach began. His love of the sea started here.

He was educated at Gordonstoun, in Scotland, where sailing was part of the curriculum. Later he took his Yachtmaster exams and lived and worked in the Mediterranean and the Caribbean both as a commercial fisherman and a freelance yacht captain.

He lives in Bideford, Devon, with his two children and devoted gundog, Finian.